DEVOTED DESIRES

STOLEN LEGACY, BOOK SIX

CANDICE BUNDY

PIPER FOX

CONTENTS

SERA IN FAELAND

I turned in a slow circle to take it all in, unable to make sense of what had happened to me. It was as if the ground were spinning beneath my feet. Tears stung my eyes, and my heart raced faster with each beat. With mounting horror, the realization sank in that I wasn't home; I was in a different world. How could this be? The portal had brought me here instead of back to my shop, Charmed Brews, despite the clear image shown through the opening.

I knew the answer. The fae Taneisha had kidnapped me and brought me here, wherever here was, against my will. I still had the auto-refilling canteen slung over my shoulder, but my clothes had been changed by the fae yet again. Now I sported a light green long-sleeved shirt with delicate embroidery running down the sleeves, comfortable dark brown hiking pants, and sturdy but stylish forest green boots. All were meticulously crafted, and while the understated style was one that I didn't recognize, I was comfortable in it.

Taneisha had deceived me. Again.

"You promised to send me home, you dirty trickster," I spat out.

How could she do this to me? I thought she respected me. Liked me, even!

Desperately searching for some way out of this nightmare, I called out. "Emrys! Franc! Caden! Marcos! Liam!" I yelled, my voice hoarse with emotion. Were they worried? Had they noticed I was gone? Had they searched for me? My stomach twisted as I stood there. The speed of my heartbeat increased, almost to the point of pain.

But all I heard was a croaking frog and the sound of wind rustling through the trees. I was in another world—and with no way to portal on my own—no way out, no way home. Alone.

I exhaled hard and tried to swallow the panic that rose in my throat. Where was I?

I knew at once that the land I stood on was enchanted. This was faery. Entirely unlike anything I had ever seen, faery looked as if they had made it from butterfly wings, cobwebs, honey, and sunlight. Spears of light fell through the forest in shafts and brushed the forest floor in glinting bars. Light streamed through holes in the canopy and fell on a multi-hued carpet of moss, ferns, and flowers.

I had read about faery back at the academy, but beyond my portal crossings in Taneisha's demesne, I had never stepped foot into faery proper before this.

"To be fair, I haven't not sent you home yet," Taneisha replied.

I turned around and found her standing behind me. She focused her brown eyes on me. Her expression was serene, her face smooth and beautiful. Her dress was emerald green with a golden sash that wrapped around her waist. She moved across the ground with a gait that made me think of a slinky cat or a fox, or perhaps both.

How could she have done this to me? I studied her eyes, but I found no remorse or guilt. Instead, they sparkled with amusement, as though she were telling a delightful secret instead of destroying my world.

I tried to sound demanding, but when my words came out, I heard the tremor in my voice. "The posse finished your quests. It's time to send me home, fae."

Taneisha's voice sounded accusing, as if I'd wronged her. "I said I'd send you home and I will as soon as I'm done with you." Her eyes narrowed and her lips twisted into a mischievous smile.

Done with me? I wondered. What was Taneisha talking about? My jaw clenched as the fear in my gut transformed into fire through my veins. "Do my mates know what you've done?"

"No! Of course not. As far as they're concerned, you walked through the portal. They even saw you walk into your shop before the portal closed. I have to thank you for asking them to give you a bit of time to yourself. That was just what I needed to keep them from becoming difficult when I separated you from the pack."

That I'd played right into her hands deflated me. "Are my guys safe?"

Taneisha drew back, appalled by my question. "Of course, silly. Your mates are back at Velvet planning a massive remodel even as we speak."

At least I could take comfort that my mates were safe, but for how long? Eventually, they'd come looking for me, but for now, I was stuck in faery with the vexatious Taneisha.

"That's some comfort. So, what's all this about? Payback for me helping the guys win back their legacies?"

Taneisha's laughter was bright, musical, and made the hair on the back of my neck stand up. "No, of course not," she said. "You're so serious! You think I did this out of spite? No, my dear. I have other plans for you."

The fear in my gut changed from suspicion to anticipation. I pinched the bridge of my nose and took a deep breath. When I had calmed down enough to trust my voice, I said, "What sort of plans?"

Taneisha's eyes twinkled in excitement as she stepped closer to me and whispered confidentially. "Simply a road you need to travel. It's so simple, I assure you. I need you to travel to a magical fountain and retrieve a potion for me."

A familiar sensation crept up my spine. "If it's so simple, why don't you do it?"

Taneisha tilted her head to the side, as though she were trying to understand a tough concept. "It's not that I can't do it, it's that I don't want to. Having you do it is much more fun."

I snorted. "No kidding. So you want me to be your errand boy?"

Taneisha grinned and nodded. "Indeed, I do. And in return, I will send you home."

I crossed my arms over my chest and considered her offer. On the one hand, it sounded simple enough. I could do it. On the other hand, who knew what sort of trouble I could get into if I were caught pilfering potion from some fountain?

"What's in it for me?" I asked.

"We've already covered that. If you succeed, I'll send you home. If you fail..." she shrugged and gave me a faint smile that didn't reach her eyes.

"You promised you'd send me home safe, Taneisha! What's really going on here?"

Taneisha heaved an exaggerated sigh, as though put upon. "If you must know, the potion I need is for a friend of mine who is cursed. I hope to lift her curse with this potion."

A friend? I wondered. I had seen no evidence that Taneisha could care for anyone but herself. But then, maybe that was just the fae in her. Maybe she had friends, and I just didn't know about them.

Or maybe she was just appealing to my compassionate side to manipulate me?

"You're sure this fountain will have a potion that can help your friend?" I asked skeptically.

"There's only one way to find out, isn't there?" Taneisha replied with an impish smile.

"Is there any penalty for stealing the potion?" I asked. "Or anything guarding it?"

"No, of course not! Come on, will you help me, Sera? Will you bring back this potion for me so I can heal my friend? I swear I'll send you home right after."

The prospect of getting home was too tempting to resist, plus, this time Taneisha had included a timeframe. I knew in my heart that I could do it; after all, I was the same witch who had helped my mates solve the fae's quests and win back their legacies. I might not be all that invested in helping the fae's friend, but I didn't see a way of getting out of faery without Taneisha's help. Perhaps I could use my magic to force her to send me home, but I still didn't trust my powers enough. Failure could mean being at her mercy forever.

Surely one more quest, and one potion, couldn't be that difficult.

"What happens if I refuse to get your potion?"

Taneisha's expression turned icy as she arched her brow. "I've promised not to harm you. Your mates, however, are another matter entirely."

The fae had been all carrot, but I'd finally found the stick. Taneisha knew I'd never risk them, sealing my fate.

With a nod, I agreed. "I'll do it. Do you have a map?"

Taneisha's smile widened, her calculated coldness of a moment before washed away as she clapped her hands with glee. "I knew you'd do it!" Taneisha said. The fae pulled a map out of a pocket on her dress, handing it over to me. "It's on the other side of the Summer Court," she pointed across the field, "so it should be a simple enough journey. I'll give you three days to get the potion."

"Three days? This is sounding like a bigger than a breadbox size quest."

Taneisha waved away my concerns. "It's through rolling meadows, along a cobblestone road, and just north past the city. Easy as pie."

I'd rather be anywhere but in faery on a random quest, but that's where I was. I already missed all of my guys, wishing they were here to help me out.

"What else can you tell me about this fountain?"

Taneisha's eyes went distant and dreamy as she recalled the history of the fountain. "It is a beautiful fountain, with several small pools surrounded by lush greenery."

"Potion. Check. Anything else?" I asked.

"Two things," Taneisha said with a grin. "First. Make sure it's the correct fountain marked on the map. There are many fountains, but only one will work. If you choose the wrong one, you'll have to make the long journey all over again. Second, you'll have to wade into the fountain. It's the only way to retrieve the potion, as it's at the center of the fountain."

"That all seems harmless enough," I said.

"I told you, it's easy. Oh, wait!" Taneisha held up her hands as if she could grab her thoughts before they flitted away. "Stay on the path and steer clear of the swamps. They're more dangerous this time of year, but I'm sure you'll be fine, because you're not even going that way. Good luck!"

I felt a surge of panic as Taneisha vanished. I was all alone in the fae's world once more. I had to find this fountain, find the potion, and get back home to my guys.

Easy, right?

THE LAND OF ENCHANTMENT

SERA

I held up the map to the light of a bright spring morning, looking for a hint of the fountain. The map was minimalist, hand drawn with just a series of lines, landmarks, and labels. It marked my current location with a 'you are here' X at the bottom of the page and the fountain colored in deep blue at the top. As Taneisha had said, it was past the borders of Summer Court and into the deep wilderness of the fae world beyond. There were no marked roads in the rural terrain, only vague paths, so finding my way wouldn't be easy. Still, I was confident that I could manage it.

I set off across the open field in the direction Taneisha had pointed, map in hand, my mind racing with all the possibilities of what could happen if I failed. I walked cautiously, my stomach twisting in anticipation. I felt like I was on the verge of some fantastic adventure, but then shook my head at my folly. Had I really become so accustomed to the fae's quests that I yearned for more?

I imagined sharing this situation with my mates, and

an almost homesick feeling crept through my belly over their absence. Caden would laugh along with me, encouraging me to embrace the adventure. Liam would shake his head ruefully, but have my back. Marcos would make sure I had the best gear and plan out the route. Franc would demand to speak to Taneisha and renegotiate terms, but then he'd strategize the quickest way through faery with me. Emrys would heal my sore feet and then exude such a confident, magnetic presence that I'd have to crack a joke just to knock him out of it.

I knew each of them loved me despite my broken magic and living outside of the supe society. Each of them accepted me as I am, as I did them. All of them would support my decision to do this one last quest, each in their own way. I also knew if they realized I wasn't at home, they'd hunt me down.

If only I had a way of contacting them, but all I had were the clothes on my back, my ever-filling canteen from the last adventure, and this chicken-scratch map. Surely, as soon as they realized I was missing, they would start looking for me. But how could they locate me in faery, a realm only the fae had access to?

I trusted they would come if they were able, but most likely, I was on my own for this adventure.

I looked for any landmarks that would help me find my way. The land was eerily quiet, and the only sound was the crunch of leaves beneath my feet. The afternoon sun beat harshly on the back of my neck, and the air smelled of dirt baked by the sun. I'd been walking for an hour, maybe two. I was beginning to worry if I had read the map wrong, especially since I had seen nothing yet that looked familiar. A warm breeze blew through the dark green trees, shaking loose dead leaves that crunched underfoot. A murder of crows passed overhead, cawing to each other. I didn't want to be alone here all night.

Suddenly, a blast of sweet, blooming flower petals filled the surrounding air, coating me in a fragrant sheen. My anxiety at being in this foreign land diminished, and I breathed deeply with contentment. A soft breeze picked up and rustled through the trees ahead, beckoning me forward. As if guided by magic, I knew exactly which way to go.

The trail up into the mountainside was rough, but I pushed onward, my heart pounding, panting as if I had just run a marathon. But as I came around the corner of a large boulder, I saw a cobblestone road, recognizing it as my path forward from the map. The road vanished into a forest where something giggled and laughed just out of sight. I pulled the map out of my pocket and looked in the direction the road was heading.

I noted I was nearing the Summer Court, and it appeared when the road ahead split, that I needed to take the right-hand path around the city proper as the fastest path to the fountain. That was fine by me. It's not like I needed to meet and get delayed by the locals. I stuffed the map back into my pocket, took a chance and started down the trail, eager to see where it would lead next.

As I walked, the sunlight filtering down through the trees cast long shadows on the path ahead, but I pushed forward. A figure appeared up ahead, dressed in a billowing white cloak and crowned with a dainty silver circlet. She moved gracefully, skirts billowing about her, revealing a sparkling gossamer gown. Two guards with helmed heads flank one side, their arms stiffly at their sides, as if afraid to move. Their hands gripped their swords, ready to draw at a moment's notice.

They each wore a billowing white cloak, the fine fabric glittering as it moved in the light breeze. The two guards were tall and broad-shouldered, their helms covering their faces. The cloaks and helms were silver, gleaming in the sun. The bottom edge of their cloaks were stained mud brown as if they had traveled upon the road for some time.

"Crap," I muttered, my momentum faltering. I supposed it was too much to ask to have this quest be a simple walk through the park. Why did quests always have to have side quests? Sure, it made for a more entertaining tale later, but after all I'd been through because of Taneisha, I just wanted to get to the point, wrap up this last journey, and get home to my mates.

Of course, these fae might not be interested in me. Perhaps they were just out for a pleasant evening stroll, but I knew I wasn't that lucky.

"Who goes there?" the guard on the left demanded, his voice as gruff as his chiseled face.

I put my hands up. "I am a traveler, and I mean you no harm."

"Name yourself," the other demanded, his voice ringing with authority.

"I am Sera Lowe," I said, hoping my luck would hold. If not, perhaps they'd kick me out, sending me back to the mortal realm and my mates.

The lady held up a hand, imperiously silencing all of us. "A human, traveling alone in the lands of the Summer Court in the full flush of summer?" The lady shook her head, her lips pursed in a grim line. "That speaks to a bit of foolishness, especially at this time of the year. Tell me, what are you doing in our lands?" she asked, her voice filled with skepticism.

I hesitated. How honest should I be? I didn't know Taneisha's reputation amongst her kind. Would dropping her name help or hinder me? A second of consideration revealed my doubts. "I'm just passing through, and I'm afraid I don't know the local customs. Have I mis-stepped?"

The other guard studied me with dark eyes. "You dare walk here unescorted? These forests are full of danger, even for fae. You are bold for a mortal."

I bit my lip, resisting the urge to blurt that I didn't want to be bold, or reckless, or a lot of other words.

"You walk with recklessness," the lady said. "Such a lovely land we have here, meant to be enjoyed by those chosen few."

I inferred I was not among that elite list.

"You may address me as Lady Alia. Although I admit I do not recognize your family name, there's something familiar about you."

Alia let the question hang in the air, and I was cautious to respond. Had she interacted with my family before? I couldn't think of many reasons mages and fae might work together or socialize, at least not amicably. I'd already shared my family name, and didn't want to give her any reason to dig more deeply into her memories.

"I'd remember meeting someone as prominent as yourself, Lady Alia, but I'm afraid I haven't had the pleasure."

Alia's eyes narrowed ever so slightly, enough that I could tell she would not let this go. "I'll get to the heart of it, in due time. I always do. For now, come," she said, gesturing to the path behind her. "We'll escort you to Court where we can discuss further."

I understood her invitation to be a demand, but I knew if I went with her, I might be stuck in faery much longer than even Taneisha had intended. But what could I do?

I gave a quiet nod and then fell into step beside Lady Alia. I glanced back at the guards, who followed close behind. I'd expected their attention to be on me, but they both gazed watchfully into the forest. Perhaps these fae genuinely had my best interest at heart?

My mind drifted back to when my mates and I were at the Heart of the Desert temple and Caden had encouraged me to use my powers to speak with the sand spirits. They had trained me in many skills back at Goldenbriar Academy, to little avail at the time because of the chaotic bent of my powers. After mating and Emrys' healing, my control over my magic had improved dramatically. I'd managed not just to talk to the sand spirits, but also brokered a deal with them to win back Emrys' golden scorpion.

Between my powers and my mating bond, would I be able to reach out to my guys from faery? What would it hurt to try? These thoughts circled through my head as we walked along the never-ending, winding path through the trees and over bridges spanning small ponds teeming with fish and other wildlife native.

As I walked silently beside Lady Alia, I gathered my focus and quieted my mind. I pondered who to contact and quickly settled on Liam. As a shifter, he was well used to speaking telepathically with other shifters, so I figured he might recognize my efforts as a genuine connection. I supposed I could have chosen Marcos, but he was so levelheaded, I figured he might be more likely write off my attempts as a flight of fancy.

I reached out with my mage abilities, attempting to use my magic and our mate bond to contact Liam. I'd attempted nothing like this before, but I understood the fundamentals from my years of training. I focused on Liam's face, his smile, and the way he felt in my arms. The image of him well and truly formed, I spoke to him in my mind. "Liam? I need you!"

I got no answer, but something tickled at the edge of my mind. A thought that wasn't mine. It felt like a brush against the back of my brain, but it vanished so quickly that I couldn't be sure it had been real.

Lady Alia shot me a look, and I realized she must have sensed something. "You fool."

"I was just meditating," I explained.

Lady Alia stopped and turned towards me. "You are fearless indeed, mortal mage. You should know our rules while you are under our protection here in faery lands. Rule number one: no mortal may carry weapons within faery lands unless they are our champions or guardsmen by right of birth or rite of passage into their ranks. Rule number two: no mortal may use magic within faery lands unless they are born-fae themselves or have earned such privilege by rite of passage into our ranks or by right of bloodline lineage. Rule number three: no mortal may harm a fae, nor may any fae harm a mortal. Do you understand?"

"Yes, I understand," I answered, although I didn't understand why a people who lived and breathed magic would have such restrictive rules for using mortal magic. "But I'm not using my magic. Not really."

But there was something... a sensation in my head like someone was listening to me from afar, but then it went away before I could be sure it was real or not. A fleeting thought in the back of my mind that I couldn't shake free of fast enough to focus on it more closely and hold on to it long enough to figure out what it meant or who might have sent it to me.

"Not really?" Lady Alia scoffed, then her eyes narrowed on me. "Who are you, really, and how did you find yourself in faery?"

I felt another nudge at the back of my mind. This wasn't as subtle as before, and I felt the zing of magic flow over my fingertips in response.

A creature roared in the distance, its cry full of hunger and need. There was a movement in the undergrowth and a crushing of fallen branches.

The curiosity in her expression shifted to concern. "Fool, you're using magic! You must stop at once."

I tried to quiet my magic, but it's like I'd set something in motion and no longer had control over its course. A ringing sensation in my ears grew and grew, my magic once again on the edge of losing control, brewing panic in my veins.

The beast roared again, much closer than before.

"I don't know that I can? I'm sorry, Lady Alia, I didn't mean any harm."

She glared at me for a moment longer before sighing and waving us onward again. "We must hurry."

I didn't know what we were running from, but when we took a turn in the path and city walls rose before us, the pair of gleaming silver gates beckoning. A handful of richly dressed fae stood outside the gates exiting a carriage, but when they saw us coming, all of them rushed inside.

Even if those walls meant my captivity, at least I'd be safer inside than out. As we sprinted along the cobblestone road, I heard claws scrabbling against the stone behind us. We were running out of time.

"Can't you use your fae magic to make it go away?" I asked, breathless.

"I can't 'magic it away,' because magic draws that beast like a moth," she explained.

That explained the guard's swords.

A sensation like a gong reverberated though my mind, sending me crashing to my knees. "I'm coming," I heard Liam utter within my mind even as a guard swept me up and threw me over his shoulder. Wave after wave of mental noise clouded my thoughts, but the relief I felt hearing his response was a balm to my heart. Liam had heard me!

Another roar echoed through the forest right on our heels, and I glanced up to see the beast descending upon us. It looked like a massive shaggy lion with an expressive, almost human face, dragon wings, and a sharp stinger of a tail. A mane of brown and red hair covered its head and its skin was pale gold, with large scales that covered its belly and paws. Its claws were long, like a lion's, but longer, sharper, and more deadly, like a dragon's.

The creature's barbed tail swiped through the air, catching one guard in the side, slicing open his leather armor. The fae fell to the ground with a cry, clutching his side and writhing in pain.

The beast raised its paw and slammed it down on him

like a hammer, then dragged its claws through his body. I cried out, watching in horror as the beast shredded the guard's body, tossing blood and viscera across the cobblestones. The beast turned back towards us, and the other guard dropped me to my feet, placing himself between me and the creature.

"Run Sera! Get to the city walls while you can," Lady Alia shouted at me.

I didn't need to be told twice. I turned and took off running toward the city walls, hoping I could outrun the monster. I heard steel on steel, followed by a wretched scream from Lady Alia. Another massive, angry roar followed, and I hoped the guard's sword had found purchase.

I whoosh of wings buffeted against my ears, and I let out a shriek as powerful talons gripped around my waist. A massive roar next to my ear preceded a sudden upward lift as the ground fell away beneath me and I sailed up into the clouds.

BACK TO NOT SO NORMAL

CADEN

The damage to Velvet was worse than I'd feared. When we'd walked back through those doors, the bar was in shambles with tables and chairs overturned, broken glass littering the floor, and various bottles of liquor smashed everywhere.

After listening to Franc swear up a storm in honor of the deceitful fae, Taneisha, we'd quickly divvied up the tasks. Franc and Emrys went to check on the staff, Liam and Marcos did a circuit of the club, and I checked on the electronic equipment.

There was no nice way to say it. The place was a wreck. The dance floor had been ground into a fine layer of glass shards. They'd trashed the DJ booth with several smashed turntables and electronics strewn about. I shook my head at the wreckage.

Franc didn't need to lose money on this mess. It was Taneisha's fault that things had gone so poorly for Franc's quest and his club. But what could we do about it? It wasn't as if we could have prevented the fae from wreaking havoc, at least not without time traveling back to our academy days and changing the ways of our past selves. It was Franc's bad luck that he had been the one Taneisha was the most angry with.

As I walked by the bar, my feet crunched on broken glass. There were several empty bottles strewn about, as if someone had flung them around in a fit of rage or drunkenness, which is no doubt exactly what happened. The door behind the counter hung open, and I peeked inside to find shelves overturned and shattered bottles everywhere.

I was pulling a trash bag out of the bin when Franc approached, laughing and talking animatedly on his cell phone. Emrys trailed along behind him, a sour expression on his face.

He hung up his call, shaking his head and clicking his tongue. "What a mess!" Gratefully, when Taneisha had returned us guys to Velvet, she'd also returned all our missing stuff, including our cell phones.

Emrys perched on one of the remaining working bar stools, leaning heavily on his elbows. The demi-god seemed to have aged a decade during Taneisha's quests, a grave weight hanging over his mood. I wondered what it might take to get him back to his normal, gregarious self.

"We'll get through it, but we're gonna need more trash bags," I replied.

Franc waved away my concern as if it would wipe away the damage, too. "I've already called two construction firms to handle the heavy work. One for rebuilding the temple and other one to remove the pond from the dungeon. I've got one coming for an estimate right now. Oh, and don't bother picking up the trash, I called a company to start on cleanup tomorrow. Other than that, it's not too bad."

"It'll be an expensive remodel," Emrys said.

Franc shrugged. "Happily, pleasure is a lucrative business. Maybe not 'ruined by the fae' lucrative, but still."

"I was kind of partial to the pond," I admitted, setting the trash bag aside.

"I've got nothing against ponds, but it doesn't work in the basement dungeon," Franc said, and then leveled me with that knowing stare of his. "I'm guessing your thoughts are elsewhere."

He was right, my thoughts were divided between our task and thoughts of Sera. "I can't stop thinking about her."

Franc leaned against the counter next to me and crossed his arms over his chest. "Me either. I know she's back at her shop and safe, but I miss her presence."

I nodded again, looking away, not wanting Franc to see my sudden tears of frustration. "Yeah, me too. I mean, after so much time together, and now she's gone? It feels so wrong."

"We shouldn't have let her go," Emrys said, breaking his silence. "At least one of us should have stayed by her side."

Franc nodded. "I admit I feel the same, but she asked for some time to herself, and we honored that. She's our mate, so I think it'll always feel uncomfortable to spend time away from her." He sighed and then shook his head as if to clear it away. "But enough of our woes! Let's keep busy, lest we become the moody emo boys we always avoided back at Goldenbriar. How about we look for anything not broken and we can set it aside?"

The sound of someone approaching interrupted our conversation. We all turned towards the door to the gardens as Liam opened it up and walked in first, followed by an antsy looking Marcos who almost looked like he'd rather be out running his panther than here at Velvet. When they saw us gathered around the counter, both headed our way.

"What's your assessment?" Franc asked.

Marcos shrugged. "The place is a wreck, but the damage is repairable. Most of it's surface level stuff. Events shook the staff up pretty bad. I'd recommend giving them some time off, but they're all safe and accounted for. There are even a few who showed up for their shifts today and are just doing clean up." He glanced at me, then Franc, before turning back to Liam.

"There's nothing unsalvageable, if you're willing to spend the money on repairs," Liam added.

"This will put me back, but I'm not giving up on Velvet," Franc replied. "And those stalwart few who showed up today are earning a bonus. Hell, who am I kidding? All of them are just for sticking with me through this insanity."

Liam's cell rang, and he took a few steps away to answer it. "Hello? Hey mom, yeah don't worry, I'm fine, really."

"Yikes," I replied. "I'd better check in with work, too. Although they likely just figure I'm too busy to call. The benefits of undercover work."

"I'm not sure my dad's noticed I've been gone," Emrys said, seeming more tired than upset about the prospect.

"No mom, I can't go on a date with Wendy," Liam said. He held the phone away from his ear for a moment, and I knew all of us could hear his mom reading him the riot act. "Mom. Mom!" he exclaimed. "I have a mate now, so you can stop playing matchmaker for me."

"There's nothing like a wolf momma's drive to marry off her cubs," Marcos muttered, shaking his head.

We shared a laugh, then continued to listen and live vicariously through Liam's phone call.

"Yes, Mom, I'll bring her by, but things are busy now. I'll call you tomorrow, okay? Okay bye!" Liam ended the call. "Why did I think telling her I had a mate would settle her down?"

"No man, now you'll get the 'when will I have grand-cubs' questions," Franc replied. "It's never ending."

Just then, Liam rocked on his feet as if a powerful gust of wind had hit him.

Marcos reached out and grabbed him. "Hey, are you okay?"

Liam nodded, holding his hands to his temples. "Yeah, I'm just feeling a bit out of it suddenly." When he swooned a second time, Marcos guided Liam over to a chair and made him sit.

"What is it?" I asked, but Liam remained quiet.

Emrys moved to him, kneeling down beside the chair. "Can I help?" When Liam nodded, Emrys ran a hand over the wolf-shifter's head, healing his headache and calming him.

Liam's eyes shot open. "I think Sera needs us."

Emrys frowned. "How do you know?"

"I'm not sure, just a gut feeling?" he answered.

"That's enough for me. We have to answer Sera's call," Marcos said.

"Agreed," Franc replied, holding up his hand.

"Assuming she's actually in trouble. How do we know she's calling for help? I mean, why didn't she just call or message us?"

"I just know," Liam insisted. I didn't blame him for being cranky over our mate's safety.

"Look, maybe she can't call? We should make sure Sera is okay." Marco's words felt like an echo of my own thoughts. "I don't trust the fae."

Emrys stood up and shook his head. "I'd also feel better if we checked in with her, even just to let her know we're here for her, but she asked for space." Emrys sighed. "She'll contact us when she's ready. If we ignore her request and push her now, we're disrespecting her."

I'd never imagined Emrys would be the one to pump the brakes, and it gave me pause. "What if we just call, or message?" I asked. "What's the most respectful way of keeping our distance while checking to see if Liam's hunch is correct?"

Emrys and I shared a look, and then we both turned to Franc. Franc nodded along with me as if confirming my thoughts were correct in his mind too.

"Let's look in on her?" Franc suggested.

"No contact? Just a visual to confirm she's all right?" I asked. My fangs ached at the thought of sinking them into Sera again. "That sounds good to me."

"Okay, but not all of us, and we have to stay out of sight," Emrys added.

"How do we decide who goes?" I asked.

"We draw straws," Franc replied, grabbing a handful of literal compostable paper straws from behind the counter. He tore off two short and then hid the ends. "There are two shorts and three longs. That way we don't go alone in case something is wrong."

Marcos walked right up to Franc and drew first. Without a comparison, it was impossible to tell whether he'd won or lost. Emrys went second, pulling the same length. Liam drew third, and then they had three matching straws. Liam glowered while Marcos returned to his pacing.

When I pulled mine, it was short. I breathed a sigh of relief. Sure, I could have swapped places with either of the shifters, who both seemed to have a hard time staying in human form knowing their mate might need them. But I'm just not that giving of a guy, so I didn't.

Franc opened his hand and showed his, which matched mine. "You three stay here and handle the temple repair contractors. Caden and I will drive by Charmed Brews and see how Sera's doing."

"You'll call us as soon as you see her?" Liam asked.

"Of course. We'll even send you pictures," I replied, my taunt earning me a low growl from Marcos.

DOWN THE RABBIT HOLE

SERA

I screamed at the top of my lungs as loudly as I could, determined to make my voice heard. "Can't we talk about this?" I begged, then took a breath to calm myself. He just held me tighter against himself with a single paw under my chin and one across my stomach and hips.

The manticore let out another deafening bellow, a blast of scorching wind that threatened to tear my clothes from my body and blow them away into the skies. My stomach lurched with each flap of the beast's giant wings, and I was grateful my stomach was relatively empty.

"Where are you taking me?" I screamed. The beast let out another ear-shattering roar and then was silent, as if contemplating my question. I tried again. "I assume that means you don't understand me? Do you even speak English?"

There was no answer, but then again, I hadn't really expected one. I tried to summon fire in my hand like I normally would. It sparked and flashed, but nothing more.

Lady Alia had said magic drew the beast. Was it also preventing mine from functioning normally, or was I unable to perform because of my fears?

"What the hell is wrong with my magic?" I demanded of the beast. Again there was no answer, but then again, I hadn't really expected one. Then again, what would I do with a fireball right about now? Convince the creature I was too much trouble, causing it to drop me? No, I needed to take another tactic. "Please put me down! Just put me down and we can forget this whole thing ever happened!"

The beast turned its massive head toward me and sniffed at me like an animal scenting its prey. Intelligent eyes weighed me, and I suspected it understood my pleas. Then he opened his enormous maw and opened his cavernous mouth wide enough to show me that his rows of teeth filled most of the space within his mouth. His tongue was long and thin like a serpent's, shifting back and forth as he watched me struggle against him. Then he snapped his jaws shut mere inches from my face while growling low in his throat.

"Fine, fine! Sorry I asked." I supposed I should be grateful my magic fizzled. The last thing I needed was for the beast to drop me from this dizzying height. "I wish you could at least tell me where you're taking me," I said to the beast, hoping to get a response. "Are we going to your lair? Your nest? Your home? Your hive? Whatever it is you call it!"

There was no answer, but then again, despite my need to try pleading with it I hadn't really expected one. I looked down at the ground, which was now a fair distance below us. I looked up at the sky, hoping for some divine intervention. No lightning bolt came crashing down on my captor.

I'd never been afraid of heights before, but as the ground swept beneath my feet, I had to admit this was a novel experience for me. I managed reaching into my pockets and dug around, grasping Taneisha's map. I pulled it out and tried to orient it to the landmarks below, only to have it whisked away by a sudden updraft.

"Well, that's an auspicious sign," I muttered under my breath.

With no other option available, I stopped fighting against the creature's grasp. The beast turned his head toward me and sniffed again at my face with his wide open mouth. Then he snapped his jaws shut close enough to blow my hair back from my face and ruffle it around like he was blowing it dry with hot air from his nostrils.

"That's not funny!" I yelled at him while struggling against his grasp again, but it was no use. I was on this carnival ride of a beast until it decided otherwise.

When the beast slowed and began circling over a river, I wondered whether I should be more afraid of what might come next. He landed gracefully on a wide, pebbled bank. There wasn't anyone or any other creatures in sight, unless I counted a mass of small, glowing orbs floating above the water's surface. Perhaps they were the equivalent of faery mosquitos? At least they seemed harmless enough.

I recalled the river on Taneisha's map; it was the only one she'd drawn on there. Could this be the same one?

The beast gently set me down on my feet, and I immediately pulled away from him. He circled around me, sniffing me, his long, serpentine tongue flicking over his lips. I took a step backwards and then another. The manticore continued circling. Was he going to eat me? Kill me? Keep me captive?

"Could you stop that?" I asked him. "I wish you could talk."

He stopped and sat on his haunches, watching me with his intelligent eyes.

"Thank you," I said with a sigh of relief.

"I wish you could at least tell me your name," I said. The monster growled and then let out another ear-shattering roar. "Okay! Okay! Nevermind!" I said to him as I held up my hands in surrender. He hadn't hurt me so far, but I was under no illusions that he could turn deadly with those teeth and razor-sharp claws, just as he'd done to the fae guard. The threat was implicit, but I supposed if someone had sent him to kill me, he'd had plenty of opportunities already. "I get it! You've got me here, wherever here is, what's next?"

The beast nodded and then turned away from me, facing the river that ran before us. His massive head dipped into the water for a moment before he lifted it back up, shaking off the droplets of water from his mane like a dog after a bath. Tiny orb creatures swarmed around him, as if drawn to him for a moment, then losing interest in him the next.

What was the story with this beast? He'd attacked Lady Alia and the guards to capture me yet for all his apparent strength and long claws, the beast hadn't hurt me. In fact, he'd taken pains to be gentle, his roar being the one notable exception.

"So, what now?" I murmured half to myself, half to the beast. In reply he growled, stood and shook his head again, then took a few steps along the river bank upstream. He paused and glanced back my way, huffing impatiently. So I was supposed to just follow him?

The thought gave me pause. Could this be a part of Taneisha's plan? If so, was she using the manticore to aid my journey to the fountain? That didn't fit her pattern from the quests with my mates, but then again, nothing the fae did was predictable.

What was Taneisha up to, really? And if not her, then what was behind this manticore's motivations?

The manticore huffed again, this time letting out a low, rumbling growl that reverberated in my bones. "Yeah, yeah. I'm right behind you, big guy," I replied.

The manticore continued up the river, and I kept pace with him. He didn't even seem to pay any attention to where he went or where he was going. He just walked.

Every so often, he'd stop and wait for me to catch up. For a predator, the beast was being pretty patient with me. Then I realized predators must excel at tiring prey out, so perhaps that alone shouldn't encourage me.

My legs burned as I walked up the shoreline. It was like running on sand, not pebbles, and my muscles were not used to the repetitive motion. Unlike the manticore, walking on the loose pebbles along the rocky shore was tiring me quickly. I stopped at a nearby tree stump to stretch my calves. The muscles loosened a bit, and I sat on the stump to catch my breath.

The river was wide and shallow here, barely a trickle of water running through the rocky bed. The manticore stayed close to the bank, his massive claws digging divots into the rocks and sand as he paced back and forth across the stream bed. He turned his head back towards me again and let out another impatient growl.

"I'm coming, Mr. Pushy!" I called out. "Just taking a moment for my legs to rest!"

The beast huffed out another breath, and I pulled myself back onto my feet, shuffling along after him. He could have easily outpaced me or even flown away, but the manticore appeared determined to get me somewhere. When I caught up with the manticore again, he continued up the riverbank until we arrived at an area with pools of water several feet deep dotting the ground in front of us. The tiny orb creatures flew up and around in beautiful swirls, and they blended together to form iridescent patterns of color. They morphed from one shape into another, their spherical bodies becoming birds and fish in midair, then transformed again into flowers and butterflies.

The manticore sat down heavily on his haunches, folding his wings tight against his body, then grunted and nodded his head toward the pools, as if urging me forward. He laid down and groomed his mane, licking his paw and then brushing it through the scruffy fur.

"You're sending me in there alone?" I asked, decidedly charmed by this gruff, grouchy, and deadly creature.

The manticore blinked back at me deliberately, as if I were the slowest person on the planet. Well, perhaps only the slowest person in faery.

I took another look across the watery area in front of me and decided it would have been better named a bog. I didn't relish the prospect of wading through the pools, especially not knowing how deep the water was. Something slithered by under the surface of the nearest pool, just out of sight.

Hadn't Taneisha warned me to stay away from the

swamp? But what else could I do with the manticore urging me forward.

"I'm not scared of snakes, mind you, but I'd feel better about it if I could see through that murk. I don't suppose the big bad kitty wants to carry me across the muddy pools?" I asked, glancing back at the manticore.

He paused in his grooming and sniffed. The beast slowly licked his bright pink tongue over his nose, like he'd scented something tasty. I wondered how Taneisha had ensnared this creature's will to her desires, and just how firmly that grip might hold.

"Don't go getting any dinner ideas, shaggy."

He let out a rumbling purr, and I held up my hand to stop him.

"No, don't you dare. You're not chasing me around this bog." He shook his head, and the ruff on his neck stood up straight. "I'd better get myself to the other side of the water," I mumbled to myself.

I walked gingerly out onto the watery surface, which was only a little over ankle deep at first. The mud and moss squished under my boots, even as the water magically supported my weight. The thick mud sucked at my shoes with each step, but it didn't slow me down much. I made it across the first pool when something slithered around my right ankle, pulling me off balance. As I fell forward towards a grassy, reed-filled bank, magic erupted from my hands, quickly stalling my momentum. Whatever force had dampened it before had now diminished, and I could gratefully step up onto the mossy embankment without falling to my knees in the mud.

I pulled my foot free of the mud, shaking off the muddy water and the creature that had latched onto me. I looked down at my boot, expecting to see a snake slithering away. Instead, it was a string of tiny balls of multicolored light. The rope-like creature slid off my boot, sliding silently back into the water.

I summoned a ball of light into my hand to illuminate the water at my feet, hoping to get a better look. As if on cue, more orb creatures emerged from the depths.

"What are you?" I asked the orb creatures, who flitted around me in a swarm. They hummed back at me, their voices blending together into an unintelligible harmony that tickled my brain in the most curious way. I let out a laugh. Of all Taneisha's quests, this one was the most curious by far. But none of the others had been in faery, a land which welcomed no mortal.

The orb creatures swirled around me, dancing in the air like fireflies on a summer night. Their numbers grew as others joined them from other pools and from the surrounding vegetation. The orb creatures hummed back at me again, flashing from one shape to another faster than I could follow.

"You're beautiful." As I spoke the words, they seemed to please them, and they swarmed around my head with their trilling song of delight before darting away across the watery expanse before me. Moments later they returned with even more who joined their ranks in circling around me, giving me an experience in this magical place previously reserved for fae alone.

My mage senses were on high alert here in faery, and my magic hummed under my skin with eager anticipation for something more than just these tiny balls of light. For what? Something more powerful? Something dangerous?

Something forbidden? I looked around me, trying to find with my eyes what my magic knew instinctively.

A flicker of movement caught my eye near a pool off to my right. When I turned to look, I saw a man standing there watching me. I froze in place, afraid to move or draw attention to myself. He was tall and slender, with long gray hair hanging loose down his back over a flowing pale silver gown that covered his frame from neck to toe but left his arms bare. His skin was pale ivory, framed by dramatic deep blue markings on his neck and arms that reminded me of tattoos or henna artistry. His eyes were a pale moonstone with yellow flecks that glowed like fire under the sunlight shining down on us both from overhead.

The fae raised his hand toward me as if summoning something out of thin air which he then hurled at me across the watery expanse between us. Silvery lines moved like lightning over the boggy, misty ground, unerringly seeking me out despite their erratic path.

Fear shot through my chest as if expecting the strike. What had I done to earn this fae's ire? Perhaps my presence in this place had violated some custom? My magic surged within me again as I raised my hands to meet this attack head-on, forming a glowing, green wall of protective energy. I could only hope my shield would hold against the fae's attack.

MISSING PERSONS

"Tell me you didn't cheat the straw pull," Caden said, his tone an accusation.

We sat in my Ford Mustang in the parking lot outside of Charmed Brews watching patrons coming and going. It'd been busy enough that we didn't have a good view to see Sera behind the counter, but it was only a matter of time before we got lucky and spotted Sera inside through the window.

"Okay," I drawled back at him. "I didn't cheat the straw poll."

Caden let out a long sigh. "Dammit man, that's not playing fair with your brothers."

"I knew it had to be us looking in on Sera," I explained, lifting my hands in surrender. "If Liam or Emrys were here, they'd never be able to stop themselves from going to Sera when they saw her."

Caden tried to hide his smirk, but I could see him smiling through his irritation. "You say that like you think we can do it? How the fuck are we supposed to keep ourselves away from her? It hasn't even been a full day and all I want is for her to be in my arms again. I want to take her home and cook something amazing for her like she is my queen or something, man. You see this crazy look in my eyes? This is love, man! Love!"

I burst into laughter. "Cooking? Really? You can't be serious! That's what you're fantasizing about doing with Sera?"

Caden smiled at me, his face lit up from within, his eyes glimmered with happiness and love. "Oh I am, brother. We really bonded over ice cream and I have some ideas involving pistachios and candied orange that sure as hell will drive her crazy."

I laughed at him, my eyes tearing up with happiness again. "Whatever floats your goat, demon," I replied. "If it makes both you and our mate happy, I'll even buy the nuts."

Caden reached over and laid a hand on my thigh, rubbing it slightly through my pants as he looked me in the eye. The look in his eyes made my shaft twitch. "And I'd even allow you to bring the nuts," he said with a smile.

I leaned in and whispered against his cheek. "I like many nuts, but I draw the line at pistachios," I admitted.

Caden pulled back, feigned horror. "You heathen!"

I inclined my head. "Definitionally."

We had a good laugh, but it wasn't long before our mood sobered. I didn't want to say anything, but every minute that passed that we didn't see Sera made me more worry more and more.

"I wish we could just walk in there and ask how she's doing," Caden said.

"Yet you know Sera asked for some space and we need to be discreet."

Caden turned toward me and crossed his arms. "You know we're sitting here in your neon pink car, right?"

I shook my head. "It's on brand for Velvet and it tops out at 160. Besides, there's a ton of cars here in the parking lot. We blend in."

"Said no one ever about our posse. It's a damn fine ride, Franc, but subtle, this ain't. If Sera walks out of that door, she'll definitely see us out here. You know we should have brought an unfamiliar car."

I groaned, running my hands through my curly hair, and then down over my face. "I get it. You're right. I should have supported Sera's wishes for space, but I was just worried about her too much. I want my mate safe and happy. If that means going against her wishes once in a while, then so be it. I'll take full responsibility and apologize later."

Caden laughed at me, shaking his head. "You are a piece of work, demi-god, but I love you anyway. You always look out for the others when they need it the most, even when they don't realize it yet themselves. That said, I think we could both use some time with our mate right about now." He turned back around in his seat, facing forward as he spoke to me again. "Should we go? We can swing back by later? Or maybe do a drive by on her house? Or not? What do you think?"

I turned my head and met his gaze with my own, then turned towards the front of the car again as I answered his question. "Let's go inside and see if she's there; after that we can take a drive by her house and check up on her."

The matter decided, we locked up the car and crossed the parking lot to Charmed Brews.

I pulled the door open and walked into the shop with Caden right behind me. We looked around, taking in the space. The scent of coffee beans permeated the air. The front room had a counter in an L shape along the right side and across the back with a row of tables and chairs on the other wall. Off to the left the space opened up, revealing table upon table with patrons boisterously drinking the shop's wares as they played role-playing games.

Behind the counter were shelves stocked with coffee mugs and bags of beans. I didn't see anyone behind the counter, but there was a door marked 'staff only' at the back. Perhaps that's where Sera was?

I caught sight of the missing person's poster in the window and walked up to it to get a better look, ripping it as I pulled it off the glass. I read it over twice before I realized what it said, my eyes continually drawn to the picture of my mate on the page. My heart leapt into my throat as I turned towards Caden, who had been waiting for me to finish.

"What does it say?" he asked me.

I held it up for him to read along with me, hoping against hope that maybe I hadn't understood what it meant the first time through.

'MISSING: Ms Sera Lowe, beloved member of our community and owner of Charmed Brews. Any information leading to finding Ms. Lowe will be rewarded. She is 5'6" tall, 155 lbs with black hair and brown eyes. She was last seen in the company of one Emrys Tedros and may still be with him or his friends, Franc Lyaeus, Liam

Grant, Marcos Wright, or Caden Zagrolun. Anyone with information on her whereabouts or the whereabouts of the men listed above should contact Detective Obras at Garda City Police Department (360) 555-1234 or Ms. Dara Lowe at (360) 898-9922.'

I stared at it for a moment, then looked up at Caden again, unable to find any words to say just then. When I found my voice, I was pretty sure my words came out in more of a whisper than anything else. "If Sera had returned to her shop, would this poster still be up?"

"I don't know," Caden replied, rubbing his chin. "Probably not."

"This means she hasn't been back here," I replied. "It's been a full day. She wouldn't have just gone home and not to her shop. She loves this place!" I paused, realizing I was ranting. "Oh, this isn't helping. Let's figure out where Sera is."

Caden put his hands on my shoulders and pulled me in for a hug. "Hey now, we don't know any of that yet. We don't even know if she knows about the poster yet or not. They might have missed taking it down in the hubbub of her return home."

I took a deep breath, clearing my thoughts. "I just need to figure out where Sera is and confirm she's okay." I looked at Caden and nodded. "Let's find Pepper, the lady Sera left in charge of the shop. She'll know where Sera is. Then we can figure out our next steps from there."

Franc nodded. "Okay."

He and I walked over to the counter and leaned against it, waiting for whoever was inside to open the door. An agonizing minute later, a tall, elegant-looking older woman, dressed in jeans and a paint-spattered t-shirt came through the staff door. Her name tag read 'Pepper.' So this was the woman Sera had left in charge of her store.

She had no sooner looked up than she called out, "Well, hello there," the warm smile she directed to us curling the edges of her mouth. "What can I get you?"

I visibly relaxed as soon as I saw her. "We were hoping you could help us," I greeted Pepper, holding out the missing persons flyer.

She looked the picture over quickly and tipped her head to the side a bit. "Are you friends of Sera's?"

Caden nodded, saying "That we are. We've been looking for Sera and we were hoping she might be here. Is she still missing?"

Pepper nodded, her expression grave. "Well, she isn't here. I haven't seen her in a couple of weeks now. The whole town has turned out looking for her, but no luck."

"You're sure no one's seen her?" Caden asked. "Just in the last day or so?"

Pepper shook her head, crossing her arms. "That's a curious follow-up question. I don't suppose you're friends with one Emrys Tedros?"

I glanced at Caden and then back to Pepper. I couldn't see the point in hiding what we were doing from her, especially if it would help us find Sera.

"We are friends of his and Sera," I confirmed.

Pepper raised an eyebrow skeptically. She didn't comment on how we knew Emrys. "If that were true, I think I would have met both of you before now."

"We just recently reconnected with Sera," Caden added. "Two days ago we returned from an unexpected trip and we thought she had headed home."

Pepper frowned and shook her head. "Maybe you

should have walked her to the door, because if she had turned up I would have known. Sera is one of the most reliable people I know. She would have checked in with me if she got home safely. I would have seen her."

Pepper's words chilled me to the bone because I knew them to be true. Sera was missing and all five of us should have been more careful. Pepper was right. We could have allowed her space after making sure Sera had gotten home safely.

"Do you have her address?" I asked, hating the fact that I didn't know where my mate lived.

"Why in the world do you think I'd give a stranger her address?" Pepper said, pursing her lips.

"Sera told us she knew you would keep Charmed Brews running while she was away and that she wished she had a way to reach out to you to let you know she was safe. She didn't worry about her family, she worried about you."

Pepper's eyes glistened with unshed tears, and her attention turned towards the door. "Anyone could say that."

"Look me in the eye," I said, again catching Pepper's gaze with my own. It was very important for me to say how much I loved Sera and how badly I wanted her to come home safe. "It's my fault, well our fault. We swept away Sera from her life these past few weeks. I swear to you, Caden and I will not rest until we get Sera home safe to you, just as we promised you we would find her. Not just anyone would make such a promise; we mean every word."

Her gaze lingered on me for a few more silent moments before she nodded her head slightly. When she nodded, my breath released in a ragged sigh. Pepper grabbed a business card from the counter and scribbled an address on the back.

"This is her apartment. It's not too far from here. I've gone by every day hoping for a sign she's back, but nothing so far."

Caden swiped up the card, reading the address. "We'll find her, Pepper. Thank you for your trust."

"I expect you to deliver, gents," Pepper replied. "Sera's family is looking for her too, and you'd do well to get her home safely before they find you."

We thanked Pepper and headed down to the car. Once inside, I started the engine and drove off with Caden navigating. We were quiet for a few minutes, save Caden's gruff directions, as I stewed in my thoughts.

Caden got on his phone, and I could guess who he was calling.

"Hey Marcos," he said into the device, putting the phone on speaker. "Sera wasn't at her work, and her gal Pepper said she hasn't shown up."

The line was quiet for a moment and then I heard the rest of the guys muttering as Marcos turned on his speaker and filled them in.

"What's the plan?" Marcos asked us.

"We're headed to Sera's apartment next," I replied.

"Makes sense. Do you have any working theories?" Marcos asked.

"She might be with her family," Liam said. "The cousins said they'd been looking for Sera. She might not have gotten back home yet if they intercepted her."

"Or Taneisha still has her," Emrys added. "Damn it.

Sera went through that last portal alone. We don't know for sure where it led."

During Emrys' quest to win back his golden scorpion, he and I had traveled into a potential future where Sera had died. As I drove, I replayed scenes from the cemetery in my mind. The conversation with her family, the tombstone, the sense of certain dread.

"Let's not jump to worst-case scenarios. We need to talk to her family. Sera's most likely with them," Marcos added.

"And we should figure out how to get in touch with Taneisha," Emrys added.

I never wanted to see Taneisha again, but if she had Sera, I'd travel to the end of the world to find her.

"Come up with some ideas. We'll call back with an update as soon as we have a look at Sera's place," I said.

Caden hung up the phone. "You need to keep it together," Caden said softly.

I gripped the wheel like a vice. "Don't I look like I've got it together?" I asked, grinding out the words.

"No. No, you don't," he replied. I shot Caden a glare, but he wasn't having it. "I know you're worried about Sera. I am too. But right now she needs us to rally and figure out what's happened to her."

I raked a sweaty hand through my curls. "I just keep thinking about that cemetery. I was so sure afterwards, after we'd avoided the temple mummies, that we'd prevented that dire future. What if I was wrong? What if the dire future wasn't anything about that temple? What if Sera's in trouble and we weren't there for her when it mattered?"

Caden gripped my shoulder. "We'll find her, Franc. We won't stop until we do."

I glanced over at him. "How can you be so sure?"

"Because you've never given up before." Caden looked into my eyes, like he could see right through me. "You always believe that things can turn around. You always believe there's a solution, even when I haven't. I learned it from you, Franc." He rubbed my shoulder, his confidence grounding my anxiety.

I nodded as I pressed on the accelerator, unable to find the words to voice my fears. I couldn't imagine a future together with my brothers without our mate by our side. We had to find Sera, and she had to be okay.

ELDER LORE

SERA

My shield held against the attack, yet the force of it knocked me back a step, and I stumbled on the uneven ground. The gnarled old faery watched me with a satisfied smile, his skin the color of wet bark and hair like tangled vines. Moss wound around his ancient form like it'd grown there over time as a second skin, in some places hanging like fabric from his wiry form. He could have been a hundred years old or a thousand. I had no way to judge.

I didn't have time to wonder at his intent before another barrage of silvery lines shot through the air, this time aimed at my face. I threw up my hands to block them, but they were too fast and too many. The intense heat from the attack singed my hair and my skin as they hit home.

I cried out in pain as they hit my arms, legs, and torso with rapid-fire precision. The agony was unlike anything I'd felt before; it felt like being thrust into a fire repeatedly with no hope of escape. It took me several seconds to realize that the silvery lightning had stopped hitting me. It was only then that I realized I had fallen to the ground and lay curled up in a ball, gasping for breath while clutching my arms against my sides.

When did that happen? What had happened? How could one fae cause so much pain? Had he meant to kill me?

"Pardon, I did not mean for you to suffer so much," said the fae as he crossed the watery expanse between us, using a rough-hewn staff for support. "I would never wish you ill upon this world or any other, Sera Lowe, but it's important for you to understand you cannot withstand my will."

Wait...what had he just said? "How do you know my name?" I asked him suspiciously as I struggled back to my feet, testing each limb before putting weight on it to make sure nothing was damaged during his attack.

"I know many things," he replied simply. "I know you," he said, pointing the staff at me. "You are the one I've been waiting for."

The fae's words, although spoken softly and almost reverently, hit me like a bucket of cold water. I looked him over again, this marsh fae that very much looked like he had the skin of a willow tree, wondering what type of fae I'd stumbled upon. "What? What do you mean? How can you have been waiting for me? I don't even know you."

The fae looked confused by my outburst and didn't answer right away. "In due time. Understand it is by fate's will that we meet here, now, in this way."

"It's always fate this, fate that," I muttered under my breath.

His hairy brows knit with confusion, but then he moved on. "It's good you understand. For now, all that matters is that we are together. But first, we need to do something about those nasty burns on your skin and hair. May I heal you?"

The fae was playing games with me, but he was also offering to heal my wounds? I felt like I was dealing with Taneisha all over again! I wasn't sure what to think about what he meant by fate bringing us together. I recognized one thing; he had the power and control to make this situation easier on me if he wanted to. So far, he hadn't threatened me and seemed upset he'd hurt me physically.

"What if I don't want your help? Can you force me against my will? Is that what fate dictates?"

He laughed at my questions as if they were silly or naïve questions posed by a child who didn't understand how the world worked yet. Which was true enough. I knew nothing about how faery worked.

"We will get along better if you do not provoke me or waste our precious time with such tiresome banter, mage Sera Lowe. Allow me to tend to your wounds, or else suffer the consequences of further injury from my hand as I wait for you to comply with my wishes."

"You could at least tell me your name?" I asked.

The old fae pulled himself up to his full height, almost matching my own. "You may call me Vedreel."

Vedreel's hand hovered over my arm, and I flinched from the expected pain. But then, to my surprise, I felt no further discomfort as he worked his magic on my wounds. Within seconds, the agony of the burns had faded away.

"Thank you" I said, rubbing my arms to help bring sensation back into them. "Can you tell me why you brought me here?"

"There are some things you need to know which only I can show you."

The manticore bellowed behind us, and I turned to watch it shake its massive shaggy head as its roar transformed into a whine.

"Oh yes, oh my," Vedreel said, fumbling in his mossy layered outfit. "Patience, Miriss!"

The manticore bellowed again, and I had to throw my hands over my ears to manage the deafening sound.

Vedreel produced a clump of something from his deep pockets that I didn't want to hazard naming, raised it to his nose, and sniffed it cautiously. He recoiled, but then nodded and threw it over to the manticore, who huffed in appreciation, gobbling it down.

My brain put two and two together. "Miriss is your pet?"

"Yes, of course. He's a very good beast, isn't he?" he baby-talked to the manticore, who let out a short bark of affirmation.

Miriss yowled something, almost as if it were talking and making sense, before turning and wandering off the way we'd arrived. I was just happy to see the fanged creature leave.

"I doubt you would have found me on your own," Vedreel continued. "I'm sure you have too much sense to wander the marshes alone."

So he'd orchestrated my arrival here? I mean, of course he had. But why?

"So, what's this about things you need to show me?" I asked him, but he didn't answer. "What's something only you, who lives in faery and who I also get the impression doesn't get out of this swamp much, know about little ole me?"

He arched his brow at me and pursed his lips as if he were a teacher admonishing a slow student. "That's the question."

Vedreel turned and crossed the marsh, clearly expecting me to follow.

I hurried to catch up, slogging my way through the sucking mud. Curiously, the fae had no issues walking through the marsh and moved as easily as I might on concrete.

"What do you think you know about me?" I asked.

"I know you are a mage of great power, yet your magic has been difficult for you to control. Am I correct?"

I had that shivering feeling run over my scalp and down the back of my neck. "Yeah, but how did you know that?" I asked.

We'd reached the far side of a pool and clambered up onto a gentle hillock. The mud fell away from my boots and I said a silent thanks for the break from the muddy marshland. A large willow tree spread overhead, its leaves shimmering and swaying in the breeze.

Vedreel turned and faced me, his expression grave. "Because it is the same for all mages with similar lineage. The magic within you is wild and feral, thus you struggle to tame it."

"How could you know that? Or even, anything about me?" I blurted out. I'd confessed my magical challenges to my mates, but otherwise my problems had been a closely guarded House Lowe secret spoken to no one. Yet this fae living in a marsh near the Summer Court in faery knew all about it? Something didn't add up.

"Clean living," the fae answered, deadly serious.

I looked him over, understanding he wasn't referring to dirt, but some temperance or abstinence that might only make sense to a fae. I let that one pass.

"How is your knowledge of my magical mayhem supposed to help me?"

"I'm taking you back to your roots," he proclaimed, tapping his staff on the ground near where the oak met the mossy ground. "So you can see the truth for yourself."

The earth at the base of the tree creaked and groaned, but then split in two, revealing a descending stairway formed from dirt and moss leading down into the pitch darkness.

I raised my eyebrows. "You're taking me to my roots?"

He nodded. "You will find the answers you seek there."

"You know I'm not a tree, right?"

"That is of little consequence."

"We're in the middle of a swamp. Won't it be all water and mud down there?"

Vedreel rolled his eyes. "Magic finds a way."

I sighed, frustrated with his enigmatic platitudes. "What if I don't want the answers you offer?" I asked, but Vedreel was already walking away, leaving me no choice but to follow him down the stairs.

By my mental calculations, I was exactly three missteps away from the quest Taneisha had sent me off on just a few hours ago. The Lady Alia, the manticore Miriss, and now the marsh-tree-fae Vedreel. Was this typical for faery, for the realm and inhabitants to waylay you at every step?

Yet Vedreel had hooked my curiosity with his tease about understanding things about my magic I never had. In this moment, my inquisitiveness far outweighed my fear. I had questions for this fae, and he wasn't getting away from me.

I followed him down into the depths of the earth, descending into what felt like a crypt or tomb. What other roots could he mean? The magic within me thrummed with energy, seeming to know where we were headed and eager for answers. A flock of the glowing ball creatures swirled around us, racing ahead of us down into the depths of the earth.

As we descended further into the earth, the air became cooler and damper. When we reached the bottom of the stairwell, a new tunnel appeared before us, leading deeper into darkness. The ball creatures lit our path, and I had to wonder if Vedreel had summoned their aid.

We walked along it for some time in silence before I couldn't resist asking more questions. "So, how long have you lived in this marsh?"

He glanced over his shoulder at me. "I am the lord of the marsh. I am its foundation, its strength, and its guardian."

"That's quite a title. You said you're taking me to my roots? Why?"

He turned back around and continued walking, staff in hand. "Because you need to see them for yourself to believe them."

I frowned, thinking over his words. Had he meant literally, or metaphorically? Either way, I didn't like how cryptic he was being with his answers.

"I have a right to know where you're taking me."

He stopped short in front of me and turned around to face me again. His expression was grave as he looked me over from head to toe. He held up his hand and spread his fingers wide apart as he counted off on them one by one with each answer he gave me.

"To the center of your magic, to the source of your power. Are you ready for that? Will you trust me?"

The sudden intensity in Vedreel made my heart race faster. I nodded at him, not trusting myself to speak just yet without revealing my anxiety or excitement at what was next within reach of us all along our journey through this labyrinth of caves beneath the swampy earth here in faery.

A QUESTION OF ABDUCTION

EMRYS

"I can't just stand around," I said. I paced back and forth in front of the bar at Velvet. So much had happened that I couldn't just wait and see what Franc and Caden found out.

In response to Franc and Marcos' call, the place was a flurry of activity as construction workers and cleaners brought in equipment and supplies to repair what Taneisha had broken. They gave Liam, Marcos and I a wide berth, no doubt to the glowering shifters who were barely keeping control over their inner beasts. All the contractors were supes, so I didn't worry about them seeing Liam's and Marcos' eyes flare yellow and green with concern for our mate. That didn't mean we wanted to be overheard.

"Well, that's good because we're not going to. We need to keep all of our anxious energy in check while we wait to hear from them," Marcos replied.

"There's a strong possibility that Sera's has spent time with her family since she returned home from the quests,"

Liam said. "I'm not letting her out of my sight once she's back with us for at least a week. Since I've been living out of town the past few years, I don't have strong contacts with the local supe community."

"I bet I can make a few calls," I replied, pulling out my phone. "I have a lot of contacts, none with mages, but I bet I can find someone who knows someone." I scrolled through numbers, wondering where I should start. "You guys have any ideas how we might get a hold of Taneisha?"

There was a heavy silence as Marcos rubbed his hand up and down the back of his neck. Liam's frown lines grew deeper, deepening the creases on his forehead. None of us wanted to deal with the fae again; doing so would mean risking our lives. However, we had little choice but to do it; the consequences might mean risking Sera again.

Marcos put his finger to his lips, a habit he had when thinking, and said, "I wonder if we could contact Goldenbriar Academy and see if their alumni department might help us out?"

Of course! The school would keep contact information for their former students. If we got in touch with them, they might help track Taneisha down for us.

After about a minute of silence, Liam said, "Let's go."

"Hold on," I said. "We're supposed to wait for word back from Franc and Caden."

Marcos frowned and then said, "Time could be of the essence."

"They asked us to brainstorm places Sera might be. If there's one thing I learned over the quests, it's that we're stronger together than apart. Now we need to hang tight and think of places she might be," I said, and then looked to Liam. "Any more mental pings?"

"What? You mean, have I felt the pull of our mating bond with Sera in my mind again?" Liam asked. He turned and stared at me with piercing yellow wolfish eyes, his nostrils flaring as if he could sniff our mate out of the ether.

I nodded, holding my tongue. Nothing good would come of baiting his wolf.

"No, not since that first time." Liam looked away. "I know my wolf is on edge; he wants to go out and hunt for her right now. I can only imagine what you two are experiencing."

"Demi-gods differ from shifters, Liam. If I focus, I can sense our connection, but it's muted. Quiet."

Marcos raised an eyebrow at me. "You don't feel the pull to seek Sera out?"

"I don't," I replied, shaking my head. "I haven't, but that doesn't mean it isn't there. It's just different for me. What about you?" I asked Marcos.

"I have felt no mental taps from Sera," Marcos said. "For whatever reason, she reached out to Liam alone."

"Perhaps she only had the strength or attention to reach out to one of you?" I added, but Marcos just frowned. Come to think of it, that wasn't the positive spin I'd been hoping for.

"I can't get the image of Sera stepping through that portal without us out of my mind." Liam rubbed his chin as he paced back and forth in front of us. "We know Taneisha controlled that portal, but why would Taneisha take our mate away from us? She liked Sera! What does the fae gain from that?" Liam asked rhetorically as he paced back and forth in front of us.

Marcos chuckled at Liam's last statement and shook his head. "That sounds like a lot of assumptions about what Taneisha might think or do based on the possibility that Taneisha took Sera."

"Taneisha sent Sera through that portal home, all by herself, and we let her," Liam repeated. "Ergo, she could have easily taken her."

I barked out a laugh. "No one lets Sera do anything. Our mage demanded we give her space and let her handle her business."

Marcos held up his hands. "Chill out, you two and stop spinning your wheels. Liam, call Goldenbriar and see what the alumni department has to say. Emrys, start your phone tree to find the Lowe clan."

"But keep it low key," Liam added. "From what her cousins said, we already know the Lowes are looking for Sera."

I crossed the dance floor and slouched down onto a mostly serviceable couch before hitting my speed dial.

"Hey, Shiloh?" I asked.

"Hey, Em," she replied, her voice immediately on the defensive. "What's up?"

Shiloh, a water elemental, had attended Goldenbriar Academy with all of us back in the day. She'd run with a real party crowd and a few years ago I'd helped heal one of her friends who'd gone overboard with some specialty supe cocktail. Pharmaceuticals were nice, but my resurrection powers never failed. Shiloh owed me a favor. A discreet one, at that.

"I need you to keep a secret. A big one."

There was a pause, and then she answered. "Of course, Em. You know I can keep a secret. What's going on?"

I took a deep breath and let it out slowly. "I'm looking for my friend, Sera Lowe, and I'm trying to figure out if she's staying with her family. Also, I can't have them knowing I'm looking for her."

Shiloh's breath hitched on the other end of the line. "Everyone knows Sera was abducted, Em. The Lowes are out in full force, searching high and low to bring their daughter back home. There's a sizable reward being offered. I'd have heard if they had found her. It's the talk of the local supe community."

None of that surprised me, except, perhaps, that even Shiloh had heard of Sera's disappearance. Also, it meant Franc and Caden's search of Sera's apartment would likely not be fruitful.

I let out a groan of frustration. "I'm sorry to hear that."

Shiloh was quiet for a few moments before she spoke. "Em, in case you don't know this, House Lowe is looking for you. They say you abducted Sera."

"What?" I asked. "What do they mean I abducted Sera?"

Shiloh blew out a breath. "I'm not sure what to make of it. I've heard the rumors, but no one is saying anything solid. Just that you were together when she went missing and they think you had something to do with it."

I snorted a laugh. "That's ridiculous. I love Sera. She accompanied me and the guys on a job, of sorts. We were all sent home two days ago, but she's gone missing. What else can I tell you?"

Clicked her tongue. I knew that sound well from our academy days, and it never boded well for me.

"You didn't answer my question about whether you were responsible for Sera going missing?" Shiloh asked, her tone flat and even. She was hunting for answers and would dig until she got them out of me.

I sighed and scrubbed my hand through my hair, tugging at the roots in frustration as I debated my answer. The last thing I wanted to do was get Shiloh involved in this mess, but time was of the essence.

I took another moment to debate my answer before answering Shiloh honestly. "No, I didn't abduct Sera or cause her any harm. If anything, someone else took us both against our will."

"Someone who?" she pressed.

I didn't want to target Taneisha, not because I was protecting her, but because I worried what might happen to Sera if the fae still had her.

"I'm not comfortable sharing who took us."

Again, an uncomfortable silence hung in the air on the line between us. "Hmm. But you're back and Sera is still missing? What do you think the Lowe's will think about that?"

I had an idea, and it placed me right in the Lowes' crosshairs. "I swear I didn't hurt Sera, Shiloh."

"You want my advice, Em?"

"Sure?" I replied, hearing the question in my voice.

"Turn yourself in to the Lowes and tell them everything you know. That, or leave town, but I bet they already know you're back, and not from me."

Shiloh's words shook me to the bone. "Thanks, Shiloh."

"Don't mention it. Like, literally."

The line went dead as I shot to my feet. Marcos and Liam were chatting as I ran up to them.

"Goldenbriar won't give out information over the phone, we'll have to go down there in person," Liam explained.

"We need to go. Now," I said, blowing past them on the way out the door.

Marcos and Liam ran after me, easily keeping pace with my mad dash towards the front door of the club.

"What'd you find out?" Marcos asked me.

"The Lowes have declared me public enemy number one. They think I'm responsible for Sera going missing," I explained.

"It's sort of true," Marcos replied.

"Shit, man. So where are we going?" Liam asked me.

I ran through the doors, skidding to stop as my eyes adjusted to the brightness of daylight. "Anywhere but here, I need time to think." I lifted my arm to block out the sun, or at least I tried to lift my arm, but my body fought me. Panic raced through my veins.

Shiloh's warning had come too late.

"What do we have here? Emrys Tedros in the flesh. I have someone who's overdue for an audience with you."

The speaker, who I didn't recognize, stepped into my field of view. The man had short, white hair that was slicked back from his forehead, giving him a severe and menacing appearance. His features were sharp and angular, with a thin nose and cruel lips. His eyes were cold and calculating, and they seemed to pierce right through me.

There were two others with him, but I couldn't quite focus on them. I tried to respond, but I couldn't move my lips to answer. Neither Liam nor Marcos replied, so I assumed they'd been frozen as well.

"How rude of me, I haven't even introduced myself." His dark robes flowed around him as he moved, and his staff crackled with dark energy. He was tall and muscular, and he radiated an aura of power and menace. He moved with a grace and precision that was almost inhuman, and his every gesture exuded confidence and authority. "I'm Erebus Ashwood, and as I'm sure you've already surmised, I'm a member of House Lowe."

Sera's grams was not fucking around. Not that I disagreed with going all out to find Sera, but I had no way of telling them this wasn't moving any of us in the right direction.

"You don't appear surprised at my arrival," his pursed lips frowned. "I'd question you here, but I require privacy to truly enjoy myself."

With a flick of his wrist, Erebus sent a cloud of dark energy flying towards us. Shadows swarmed around us, and my entire world went black. I was powerless to do anything but go along for the ride.

UNDERCOVER LOVERS

FRANC

I parked in the visitor parking lot and then Caden and I walked over to Sera's apartment building. We slipped through the front entrance as another tenant was leaving and took the stairs up to Sera's floor, where I knocked on her door. There was no answer. I knocked again, but no one answered.

"She must not be here either," Caden said. "I can check outside to see if there's a good view of her balcony? Might see something inside that way too."

I nodded, and he headed off down the hall. I knocked again, this time listening carefully for movement inside the apartment. My gut told me something was wrong with Sera, but I couldn't tell if it was my demi-god intuition or just the fear of not being able to find her running through me.

The door across from Sera's opened a crack, and an older woman peeked out at me. She looked like she was in her sixties with salt-and-pepper hair tied up in a bun on top of her head. Her eyes were a remarkable, vivid green the color of moss. "Another visitor, eh? What are you doing here?" she asked me in a gravelly voice as she pulled the door open further, revealing herself to be taller than me by several inches. "Are you family too?"

"No," I said, not wanting to divulge too many details to the nosy neighbor. "I'm a friend of the family. I'm Franc."

She crossed her arms over her ample chest and tilted her head to the side. "Call me Eloise. There have been several people banging on her door at all hours. I know they said she's missing, but I'd think if she found her way back here she'd know enough to call her family too."

I glanced down the hall, but there was no sign of Caden yet. "Sadly, she's still missing," I replied.

Eloise clicked her tongue. "She's a gorgeous girl, so I'm not surprised people are going all out to find her, but this is ridiculous. That cousin of hers, Mikael, was just here."

"How long ago?" I asked.

"Ten minutes? Fifteen? You folks need to learn a thing about canvassing an area, that's all I'll say." She pursed her lips at me and then looked over my shoulder down the hall at Caden who was just arriving back at the door to Sera's apartment. "From what I gathered from our brief conversations, Mikael seems convinced that Sera is in danger? He also said I should be on the lookout for unsavory characters. That wouldn't be you two, now would it?" Eloise asked us directly, her no-nonsense tone brooking no argument or dodges from us on the subject. "Are you folks unsavory?"

I glanced over at Caden who just shrugged at me as if to say he hadn't been able to find out anything from his brief excursion outside Sera's balcony. Eloise arched an eyebrow at me again, but then she looked past me at Caden as he joined us in the hallway outside Sera's door.

"We're just friends who want Sera found, and it sounds like we've struck out again," I said to Caden. "Sorry, ma'am, we'll get out of your hair."

Eloise looked us both over again, no doubt so she could report us to the next person, and then shut the door.

"I guess we should tell the others," I said.

"There's one more thing I'd like to check," Caden replied, pulling something from his pocket. As I watched him he unrolled a small kit of tools, selected a couple of items, and then went to work on the door.

"You can lock pick?"

Caden nodded, his focus almost entirely on the lock. "I even got work to pay for my training and tools."

"Clever trick, detective. Where did that kit come from?"

"I had a few things I kept in your back office at Velvet and picked it up while you were sorting out the contractors."

"Of course you did," I replied.

I heard the lock click open, and a moment later Caden was pulling me into the dark apartment after him. He closed the door quietly behind us. "I hope the nosy Ms. Eloise wasn't paying attention just now."

Caden nodded. "Doesn't matter. We won't stay long, I just want to make absolutely sure Sera hasn't been here."

Despite the dim lighting, I could see the layout of the room. The apartment was divided into two main rooms, this living space and a bedroom, with a small but well-appointed kitchen and bathroom off to the side.

There were a few pictures on the walls, but nothing

that stood out as particularly Sera-esque. Her couch was clean, with no throw pillows or blankets strewn across it. A few candles sat on one shelf along with some books, but that was it. Sera wasn't an overly sentimental person.

I'm not sure what I'd expected to find in her home? Some sign that she was still here, or at least had been? A scrap of paper with one of our numbers on it? Something that would point us in the right direction? Anything at all would have been helpful at this point.

My gaze fell onto a single framed photo sitting on a shelf by itself against the wall. "What is this?" I asked Caden as I picked it up for a closer look. It was just one shot of Sera with what I assumed was her grandmother standing side by side in front of a lilac bush, both wearing gardening gloves and holding up bouquets of flowers.

Caden walked over to me and lifted it from my hands, his expression thoughtful as he looked at it over his shoulder while he walked back over to the door leading out into the hall again. "It looks like Sera and her grandmother gardening together," Caden said. "I think they do it every year for Ms. Dara's birthday or something? They call it Dara Day or some such thing?"

"How do you even know that?" I asked, suddenly a smidge jealous that the demon knew something about Sera that I didn't.

Caden winked at me. "Pillow talk, babe. Never a better time to draw someone out."

"You're incorrigible, if predictable." I sighed. "I'm not seeing any recent signs Sera has been here. Do you?"

He shook his head. "We should head out and call the guys."

We were almost out the door when we heard a key in

the lock. Caden and I shared a panicked glance, then we moved on silent feet to the balcony outside Sera's bedroom. Caden closed the drapes behind us and then slid the glass door almost all the way closed.

I held my breath, straining my ears to hear what was being said inside the apartment.

"Another day, another wellness check. She's still not here," a female voice said.

"You didn't expect otherwise, did you?" a male asked.

"No. She's been gone long enough, I'm beginning to worry she'll never show up."

"Don't say that to the boss lady," the guy replied.

"I'm not the slow one, that's you," she snipped back, and her partner chuckled in response, but didn't argue. "We should still keep looking around. I don't want to miss anything by being overly hasty."

The door to the bedroom opened, and I heard footsteps coming in our direction. Caden and I both tensed, ready to make a run for it if need be. But then there was a loud crash, and the footsteps halted.

"What was that?" The female voice asked sharply.

There was a pause and then the male associates replied. "I knocked a book off the shelf in the living room."

The woman sighed and said, "Just be careful, okay? We don't want to draw any attention to ourselves here or break anything of Sera's. C'mon, let's finish up our search and get out of here before any of the neighbors report us. Again."

We waited until we heard the door close before we dared move again. Caden let out a sigh of relief, pointing at the decorative rock facing on the wall next to us.

"You're kidding me?" Did the demon really think we

could scramble down that wall? At least we were only on the second floor.

Caden arched his brow, taunting me, despite our precarious position. "Too much for you?"

A dare? Damn, but the demon knew how to bait me. "I followed you through the Netherworld, I think I can handle a few feet of down climbing."

Despite my nerves fighting for mental airtime between worries of falling and hyper-vigilance around being caught, we both made it down the wall unscathed. Caden grabbed my hand as we took off down the street, not stopping until we were sure no one was following us.

We ducked into an alleyway and leaned against the wall to catch our breath before Caden finally spoke up again. "That was too close for comfort! Do you think they're Ms. Lowe's people?"

"They had a key, so I'm guessing yes," Cade replied. "Besides, they referred to a boss lady, and they both sounded scared of her. Tracks for what we know of Ms. Lowe."

I pulled out my phone, surprised to see a message from Liam on it which I'd missed. When I pulled it up, it read: With Lowe. No Sera. Watch Out.

Caden and I exchanged a worried glance. I dialed Liam's number and waited as the line rang and rang, but it eventually flipped to voicemail.

"The Lowes took them," Caden said as I hung up the phone.

"We need to find them," I said, hearing the urgency in my voice. "We can't let Ms. Lowe get away with abducting them."

Caden nodded in agreement. "But where do we start?"

"We don't stand a chance of liberating the guys from a family of mages. We need to find Sera, and as far as I figure we're down to one last option."

"Taneisha," Caden replied, as if reading my mind. "But how do we find her?"

We both pause for a moment, considering our options. Then it hit me. "Let's go see Ray. He might have some ideas."

"Ray as in Raymond, the minotaur?" Caden asked.

I nodded. "Ray and Taneisha dated for a time, so it stands to reason he knows where she lives or how to get ahold of her. If we can find Taneisha, we can demand she return Sera."

Caden snapped his fingers. "Ray said he ran a meditation retreat, The Chillax Center."

I looked up the address as we made our way back to my car. "It's a little way out of town, but it's only about an hour away."

"Faster the way you drive," he said, grinning at me.

Caden's upbeat mood helped to lift my own, and I flipped on the radio as we drove, needing a distraction from my thoughts in the form of a boy band beat. I sped along the route to the Center hoping Ray would help us. Hoping he'd know where to find the fae that'd become the bane of my personal existence. We had to find Sera before it was too late, before Ms. Lowe did whatever mages do to extract information out of those who'd earned their displeasure.

When Caden and I arrived at The Chillax Center, an expansive metaphysical inspired retreat, I turned off my radio and immediately heard chimes ringing in the wind. We parked before the sprawling collection of buildings, each with their own unique purpose. As we walked up to the entrance, I heard birds singing in the trees and saw a rainbow of butterflies fluttering around us. We followed the path that led through the center, winding past meditation gardens and labyrinths until we came to a large open area with several benches and a gazebo in the center.

That's where we found Ray. The minotaur was meditating in the middle of the gazebo, surrounded by candles and incense. His horns gleamed in the soft light of the setting sun and he seemed more like a mythical creature than ever before.

I cleared my throat to announce our presence and Ray opened his eyes, turning towards us with a peaceful smile on his face. "Caden," he said warmly. "And Franc." His voice was like velvet as he spoke our names.

"We need your help," I blurted, before Ray could get up from his meditation spot. I explained what had happened to Sera and asked if Ray knew how to find Taneisha or where she might hide a captive mage friend, assuming she had her.

Ray sighed heavily and nodded slowly as he considered our request. "I don't know for certain where Taneisha is right now," he said finally, rising from his seat on the ground. "But I can offer my help in finding her."

A SIMPLE QUESTION

EMRYS

We arrived at the estate in a haze of darkness and I could feel the tension in the air. The henchmen dragged us inside and down a long hallway that seemed to stretch on forever. I could hear muffled voices, but I couldn't make out what they were saying.

The room that the hallway opened up into was a grand space, with walls made of solid stone and adorned with elaborate tapestries and magical artifacts. The polished marble floor and the high vaulted ceiling with intricate carvings and gilded details set an imposing tone. In the center of the room stood a large wooden table, its surface gleaming with wax, adorned with ornate candelabras and other expensive decorations. Around the table were several plush velvet chairs intricately carved with magical symbols. The room was clearly within a luxurious mansion on a vast estate, and its opulence was a testament to the wealth and power of the mage who owned it.

Ms. Dara Lowe was a formidable presence in the room,

with her graying long dark hair and piercing brown eyes. She sat at the head of the table, her posture straight and her expression stern. Her reputation as a ruthless businesswoman preceded her, and the henchmen standing guard near the door only added to the intimidating atmosphere. A younger woman stood next to Lowe's chair, no doubt her elder's assistant. Despite Lowe's haughty demeanor, I knew she had to be deeply concerned for her missing granddaughter, and no doubt willing to do whatever it took to bring her home.

The henchmen pushed us into chairs and stepped back to stand guard near the door. Erebus remained close, standing just behind our chairs. Suddenly, I regained the ability to move my hands, and I sensed Erebus had released the magical hold he'd had over my ability to speak or move. Yet, I said nothing, not yet, since I knew he could clamp back down on us at a moment's notice.

Ms. Lowe's gaze swept over the three of us, and she pursed her lips in disapproval before she spoke.

"I'm sure you're all wondering why I've brought you here," she began in an icy voice. "I'm looking for my granddaughter, Sera Lowe, who was taken from me against her will." She paused for a moment before continuing in a softer tone, "I believe one or more of you know something about her whereabouts."

My stomach clenched with fear as I realized where this conversation was heading. I knew there was no way we could hide our involvement with Sera from Ms. Lowe; she had eyes everywhere and knew more than most people gave her credit for. All we could do was hope that she would understand our situation and forgive us for our part in Sera's disappearance. She didn't yet know we were

Sera's mates, and I had to hope that when she found out, nothing we'd said here today would sour our potential future relationship.

Ms. Lowe's gaze settled on me, and I felt a chill run down my spine. "You look familiar," she intoned, her voice cold and calculating. "Nice work finding Tedros and his accomplices, Erebus," she said to her henchman, but her eyes never left mine.

"It was my pleasure, ma'am," he replied, his voice like slick oil. "Although, from the reports, there were two others in the group that slipped through our fingers."

"Not for long, I trust?"

"You can be assured. I have faith Braden and his team will be successful."

If only we could warn Caden and Franc that the Lowe clan had us, but that wasn't an option right now. It was too bad both shifters were here, otherwise we'd have been able to attempt some long-distance telepathy. I tried to remind myself that Ms. Lowe, her minions, and the three of us were all on the same side, even if they didn't know it yet.

Ms. Lowe's eyes remained locked on me. "I hope you'll forgive me for this little abduction, but turnabout is fair play, after all. I want answers, and I want them now," she said in a steely voice. "I know Sera was last seen in your company, Mr. Tedros, and while you and your friends have returned home safe, she has not."

I hesitated. Where did I even begin? Hey, Ms. Lowe, it's great to meet you? I'm Sera's mate, well one of five. Can I call you Grams too?

From the look in her eyes, Ms. Lowe would skewer me if I didn't tread carefully. Heck, she might skewer me if I told her the truth.

"It's a simple question, demi-god," Ms. Lowe continued. "Where did you take Sera?"

I sighed, knowing whatever I told Ms. Lowe, that it had to be the truth. Some mages could discern lies, and I had to assume at least someone within the powerful Lowe family had that gift. Regardless, if I wanted her to believe me, I needed to be honest.

"Respectfully, that's less important than where she is now."

Her gaze narrowed on me. "You admit you know where Sera is right now?"

"We're not positive," I replied, casting my gaze to Liam and then Marcos, who sat to either side of me. "But our best guess is that the fae, Taneisha, has abducted her."

Ms. Lowe's expression changed from one of icy anger to one of surprise. "Taneisha?" she said, her voice barely a whisper. She gestured to her assistant, who nodded and wordlessly started tapping into the tablet she'd been holding. "The name's not familiar to me. But why? What would a fae want with Sera?"

"The fae had a grudge against my friends and I which Sera agreed to help us out with. We think Taneisha still has her."

Ms. Lowe raised a finger to interrupt me. "Who exactly is this 'us' you refer to?"

"Myself, Liam, Caden, Franc, and Marcos," I replied. "We'd offended the fae while at Goldenbriar Academy, so she sought retribution against us."

"You five got in trouble with this fae and Sera willingly helped you out? I find it hard to believe she'd help you ruffians."

"Willingly, yes, but I talked her into it. Sera owed me a

favor from our school days, and I told her I'd consider it honored if she helped mediate things between Taneisha and us."

Ms. Lowe arched her brow. "At least you're not sugar coating it. Now I know how she ended up in the company of two shifters, two demigods, and a demon. I swear, when Erebus told me she was last seen in the company of the five of you, I thought he was just telling a bad 'so I walked into a supe bar' joke." I glanced back at Erebus, but he wasn't laughing. Or even smiling. Did he even know how to smile? "Let me see if I have this right. You coerced my granddaughter along on your shenanigans and then this fae took you where?"

I winced at Lowe's use of the word coerced, but then again, I supposed I deserved it. "Taneisha portaled us to her fae demesne. Sera attempted to negotiate with the fae on our behalf, but Taneisha wouldn't see reason. Taneisha offered to send Sera home, but she stayed with us."

Ms. Lowe frowned deeply. "To honor her owed favor to you, no doubt."

I shook my head. "No, she'd already tried to help me, and I wasn't holding it over her head."

Ms. Lowe's gaze lingered between Liam, Marcos, and myself and then gave a brief nod. "I sense the truth in your words. So why did my granddaughter stay with you?"

I wasn't sure what to say next, instead I leaned forward and placed my arms on the table as I thought through my response and how much I wanted to share with Sera's grams.

It was Liam who spoke next, his voice carrying a heavy gravitas. "In part, Sera missed the supe community. She saw this foray as an adventure that might fly under the radar with her family."

Marcos cleared his throat, and then added, "Sera made it clear she'd lived in isolation ever since she'd left Goldenbriar. She craved the adventure."

I had to wonder, did all the Lowe clan, including those in this room, know why Sera hadn't been active with the supe community? Had her inability to control her magic been common knowledge with everyone in house Lowe, or just key people like her grandmother?

Ms. Lowe's gaze shifted between us, her expression unreadable. "I take it then that you three have gotten close to my granddaughter."

We all answered at once, a chorus of "Yes ma'am's" and "Yes, we have's".

"All five of us," Liam added, his heated tone making the intonation clear.

Ms. Lowe nodded slowly, her gaze still shifting between us. "I see," she said after a moment of silence. "Tell me then, what did my granddaughter tell you about her magic?"

I exchanged glances with Liam and Marcos before I spoke up. "We learned Sera had powerful magic, but she couldn't control it."

Ms. Lowe's eyes widened in surprise and then narrowed in suspicion as she looked at me. "Sera freely admitted this to you?" She asked, her voice tight with emotion.

"Yes ma'am," I said, not wanting to make her any angrier than she already was by telling the truth about Sera's confession to us about her magical challenges. "There were several times on our adventures when Sera used her magic to aid us, and it was clear it wasn't easy or without complications for her. At least not at first."

She let out a heavy sigh and shook her head before standing up from the table and walking over to the window overlooking the gardens outside of the house. She stood there for a moment before turning back around and facing us again with an unreadable expression on her face.

"Wait, you said 'not at first.' Explain."

"That's correct," I replied, loving the curiosity lighting up Ms. Lowe's eyes. "Through the course of our time together, Sera's magic became easier for her to manage."

"Interesting. Do you have any idea what might have changed?"

Oh, I had my theories, but I'm not sure 'enough mates to blunt the wild edge of Sera's fire and bleed off the excess' was an answer I was willing to deliver to her grandmother. "I'm sure I wouldn't know. I'm no mage."

A ghost of a smile played over Ms. Lowe's lips. "I'd wager cheeky is your default mode, Mr. Tedros. I'm not a fan, and you're lying."

And yet her smile remained, so I held her gaze and my tongue.

"You're determined to keep Sera's secret?"

"No." Marcos spoke up for the first time. "It's her tale to tell."

Ms. Lowe appeared taken aback. I didn't imagine she often heard the word no.

"So protective of you, considering you all dragged Sera into danger."

I could see both Marcos and Liam's hackles rise at the insinuation that they'd endangered our mate, and so did Ms. Lowe.

"Ma'am," Ms. Lowe's assistant interrupted. She'd been busily tapping on her device ever since we'd mentioned Taneisha's name. "There's a Taneisha who's a subject of the Summer Court. I have reached out to your associate there, the Lady Alia, who will receive you now."

"Oh goody. Lucky us," Ms. Lowe replied, and I sensed she didn't have any great fondness for the fae either. "Good work, Prudence, as always."

"Ma'am," the assistant replied, hiding her smile.

"Erebus, make them comfortable until we return," Ms. Lowe replied, waving her hand in our direction, dismissing us. She moved toward the door, her retinue of the assistant and her guards falling into line behind her. "Don't worry, it's not jail, but I insist you remain here until we return with Sera."

I jumped out of my chair, moving to join Ms. Lowe. "I swear we'll answer all of your questions, but please let us help you look for Sera." Marcos and Liam stood at my side in solidarity. I let out a slow breath, knowing I was about to take an enormous risk. "We're stronger together."

"You're not in charge here, playboy, and I have all the strength I need without you troublemakers."

"We'll do anything, just let us help," Liam added.

Ms. Lowe's brow arched. I'd like to think we'd all learned a thing or two about over-promising, but at least Sera's grandmother wasn't a fae.

"Anything," I repeated.

"I'd advise against taking this one at his word," Erebus spoke, his voice grating over my ears. "My research says he can't be trusted to keep any of his commitments."

I wanted to snap back at him, to tell Erebus that he was wrong, that I'd changed, but I held my tongue. I couldn't defend myself against my past. Ms. Lowe would either believe me based on the truth of the words I'd already spoken or she wouldn't. My heart raced as I watched Ms. Lowe closely, waiting for her to decide. I had no idea what she was thinking, but the silence stretched on for what felt like an eternity before she finally spoke.

"It appears the playboy learned a few things over the past few weeks as well. Fine," she said, looking us all in the eye. "I can see that you are genuinely concerned for Sera and her safety. I will allow you to join me in this search, on one condition."

We all nodded eagerly, eager to prove ourselves worthy of her trust.

"You must swear an oath of loyalty to me and my family before we set out," she said firmly. "If you will do this, then I will accept your help in finding Sera and bringing her home safely."

We all exchanged glances before nodding again in agreement. We had no choice but to agree if we wanted to find Sera—we had no other leads and no other way of tracking down Taneisha or finding out where she had taken our mate. Besides, as Sera's mate, swearing loyalty to her entire family didn't seem like much of a stretch.

Ms. Lowe nodded curtly and stepped forward to take each of our hands as we swore our oaths of loyalty and promised that we would do whatever it took to bring Sera home safely.

Once the oaths were made, Ms. Lowe turned briskly on her heel and strode out of the room with Prudence at her side, leaving the rest of us standing there feeling a mix of relief and excitement at the prospect of finally being able to find Sera and bring her home safe and sound.

"Now, we're off to meet Lady Alia before she plays the fae and changes her mind," Ms. Lowe said.

We followed along behind her with a scowling Erebus bringing up the rear.

"Where are we meeting the fae?" Marcos asked.

"At the Summer Court, of course," Prudence replied.

"Oh great," I muttered. "faery again."

"What will one last trip through the portal hurt us?" Liam said under his breath.

"That's not funny," Marcos added. "But I'd walk through hell again for Sera."

"We can hear you," Ms. Lowe said from the front of the line. "And I definitely want to hear that entire story later."

YOU LIGHT UP MY LIFE

SERA

The underground chamber was like something out of a dream. Everywhere I looked, the walls glowed with bioluminescent creatures, their soft light filling the space with a gentle warmth. I could feel the energy of the place, and it was at once familiar and alien.

Vedreel motioned for me to come closer to him, and I stepped forward tentatively. He reached out to me and placed his hands on my shoulders and closed his eyes for a moment before speaking in a low voice that seemed to reverberate off the walls.

"This is where it all began for you, Sera." He opened his eyes and looked into mine. "It's where your magic was born."

I stared at him in shock, unable to comprehend what he was saying. Could he be serious? Was he telling me that my magic had its roots here?

Vedreel nodded as if he could read my thoughts. "Yes, it is true," he breathed. "Your power comes from here." He gestured around us at the magical chamber and I felt my heart beat faster with anticipation.

"What do you mean?" I asked in awe.

"It's hard to explain," Vedreel said with a sigh, "but suffice it to say that your power is connected to this place in ways you can't begin to imagine." He smiled slightly as if he had some secret knowledge that he wasn't divulging just yet.

I felt a thrill of excitement course through me as I wondered at his words. "I don't understand. How is my magic tied to this underground cave?"

"It's not the cave itself, girl. The cave magnifies the heart of your power, as if under a giant magnifying lens."

I shuddered as a sudden chill breeze found the back of my neck. Was I the bug in his metaphor?

"The earth here is the magnifying lens?"

"Yes," he winked. "But not the earth you're familiar with. This is the soil of faery. It is a magic made firmament." Vedreel took a step back, raised his staff, and struck the ground in front of me.

The ground trembled beneath my feet, and I felt the energy from the cave intensify. A brilliant light shot out from the ground and surrounded me, enveloping me in its warmth. I gasped as a voice echoed through my mind, an ancient voice that seemed to come from deep within the earth itself.

"You are one of us," it said in a low, melodic tone. "Our power runs through you like a river across the land."

I felt my heart skip a beat as I realized what was happening. What the voice meant and what Vedreel had been hinting at. I was part Fae! No wonder my mage magic had never worked like expected—it was because it had been bound up with my Fae power all along!

The energy in the room grew and grew, and in response, my magic flared into life. My body glowed with power and eerie green flames danced along my fingertips.

Vedreel stepped forward and placed his hand on my shoulder, offering me comfort and strength in that moment. He smiled softly at me before turning to face the cave wall.

"Sera Lowe," he said in a loud voice, "Welcome home."

I felt tears prick my eyes as I felt the truth of his words in my bones—in this enchanted place where for once my power didn't feel overwhelming or out of control.

"Wait a second, if I'm part fae, then my parents aren't really my parents?"

"Well, one of them certainly isn't, but now is not the time for that discussion. Now, you face a test you must pass before you may return home."

Yup. I was definitely the bug.

I gulped, feeling the enormity of the task ahead of me. I did not know what kind of test he was asking me to pass, and the thought of it made my stomach churn. I felt a wave of anxiety wash over me—what if I failed? Would I be stuck in faery, or this cave, forever?

But then Vedreel smiled at me and said, "You can do this, Sera. You have more power than you realize." His words gave me courage, and I squared my shoulders and nodded.

Vedreel stepped back and clapped his hands together three times in quick succession. The cave glowed with a brilliant white light that illuminated every corner of the chamber.

He then threw his arms out wide and shouted in a booming voice, "The test is simple—you must prove your strength by harnessing the raw power of faery."

I felt a thrill course through me as I realized what he was asking me to do. With a deep breath, I closed my eyes and focused my energy on the cave which shimmered as faery energy filled the space, and I felt an electric charge run through my body as I channeled it into myself.

Suddenly there was a loud crack, and I opened my eyes to see that the walls were now glowing with an intense green light. It was breathtakingly beautiful—the magic radiating off them was like nothing I had ever seen before!

The power coursed through my veins, threatening to overwhelm me. It was like a storm raging inside my body, and I could feel the energy surging through me. My skin felt like it was on fire, and every breath was a struggle. I wanted to scream, but my voice wouldn't work. I felt like I was going to burst apart, and I was sure that this was it— this was the end.

But then something strange happened—I felt my body and mind acclimate to the power. I let go of my fear and embraced the power, allowing it to fill me up and become a part of me. I felt a wave of peace wash over me as I surrendered to the weight of it. The energy grew brighter and brighter until it was blinding in intensity.

My eyes flew open as I realized what was happening. The power didn't feel chaotic or overwhelming anymore; instead it felt like an extension of myself, like a part of me that had been missing all along. The walls glowed brighter than ever before, and I could feel the energy radiating from them in waves.

With a deep breath, I focused my energy on controlling

the power rather than letting it control me. Slowly but surely, I gained control of it—the flames dimmed until they were just a soft glow, and my skin cooled down. I held out my hands in front of me, focusing on channeling the energy into a single point in front of me. It seemed impossible at first, but soon I could see a brilliant green orb forming in front of me.

The energy responded to me like I'd been born to it, as I apparently had been.

The walls dimmed and Vedreel stepped forward with a proud smile on his face. "You have done well, Sera," he proclaimed. "You have harnessed the power of the Fae and you have proven yourself worthy of retaining the powers you possess." He stepped back and bowed his head in respect.

I felt a wave of emotion wash over me as I realized how far I had come. Not long ago I was struggling to control my powers, but now I'd done it with ease. It was an amazing triumph—one that I wanted to savor.

But there was something I wanted even more than cherishing this hard won victory. The revelation about my paternity needed some further digging, and pronto. Neither my mother nor grandmother had ever disclosed to me who my father had been, always demurring that he simply was 'no longer in the picture.' It'd driven a wedge between my mother and I, such that we rarely spoke anymore except at family gatherings.

"Thank you, Vedreel. I wouldn't have discovered any of this without your help. Now, do you know who my father is?"

MINDFUL MINOTAURS

CADEN

Ray headed down a wide path on his meditation center's grounds while Franc and I followed along. I wasn't sure if he was headed to his car, toward his phone, or where we were going. The minotaur had said he'd help us find Taneisha, so at this point I'd follow him about anywhere if we found Sera at the end of this winding path.

As we walked, Ray shared his wisdom about relationships and the importance of understanding and acceptance. "Love is an ever-changing thing," he said. "It can't be forced, it can't be controlled. It's a living, breathing creature that needs to be nurtured."

He paused to pick a flower from the side of the path and twirled it between his fingers as he continued talking. "It takes patience and compromise to make a relationship work," he said. "Your mate and your brother-mates will have different views on certain things, but that doesn't mean you can't listen and understand each other's perspective."

I nodded in agreement as Franc asked Ray how he had learned so much about relationships. I knew Franc was humoring him, but I didn't mind the distraction. Whenever my thoughts drifted back to dwelling on not knowing where Sera was, my gut churned with concern for her safety.

Ray smiled fondly at the memory before continuing on his way with us. "I've been fortunate enough to have some wonderful people in my life who have taught me many valuable lessons," he said simply. "But ultimately it comes down to being willing to learn from your mistakes, love unconditionally, and accept one another for who you are."

We followed Ray down the winding path for what felt like an eternity. He seemed to know exactly where he was going, but an inkling of suspicion crept into my thoughts. After all, he had been dating Taneisha not too long ago, and I didn't trust him completely. Would he pick helping us over his former lover?

Finally, we reached a clearing in the woods and Ray stopped abruptly in front of a large oak tree with an intricate carving on it. "This is my secret door to Taneisha's realm," he said simply as he pressed his hand to the wood. "She created it while we were dating for ease of access, and then she left it active in case I changed my mind and wanted to see her again. But you gotta have boundaries, am I right?"

I recalled the conversation I witnessed between the two of them back at the maze. It was clear Taneisha had crossed multiple lines with Ray by abandoning him in the maze, and maybe even before that. I couldn't help but be curious where they had left things after we'd parted.

The tree opened up to reveal a hidden passageway that

led through darkness. Ray strode confidently forward, obviously at ease in this realm. Franc and I exchanged glances before cautiously following along after him together. After all, we'd come this far. What other option did we have?

We followed Ray through the narrow tunnel until we finally emerged into another clearing filled with lush flora and singing birds, most of which were subtly different, but some were the same as the forest before. Were we in faery or some realm Taneisha alone controlled? Across the clearing was a tall, rough-hewn stone wall with another ornate wooden door. As we crossed the space the moss-covered earth beneath us seemed to respond to our presence, cycling through a rainbow of colors as if in welcome to our arrival.

I assumed the artful welcome of this place was intended for Ray alone. Although we'd known they'd dated before, this spoke to a depth of connection I hadn't quite grasped. It was clear Ray and Taneisha hadn't just dated, this realm was symbolic of the middle ground they'd taken to build a life together. It took commitment to create this connected in-between land.

Ray knocked on the door and we waited in tense silence a few steps behind him. I didn't know what to expect, but after the last few weeks, I was ready for anything. A few moments later, Taneisha opened the door with a smirk on her face. She was wearing a long purple dress that matched her eyes and she'd swept her hair back into an intricate braid.

"Well, if it isn't my favorite horny beast," she said, arching an eyebrow at Ray. "To what do I owe this honor?"

Ray cleared his throat and stepped to the side,

revealing Franc and myself behind him, and Taneisha's broad smile faded, replaced with a scowl. "We're here to ask for your help," he said firmly.

"We?" Taneisha said, her eyes flashing with anger. "What are you two doing here?" she spat out.

I stepped forward and met her gaze evenly. "We're here for Sera," I said calmly. "We believe you know where she is." I didn't say that I also believed Taneisha had abducted Sera. It might have been true, but we needed the squirrelly fae to help us.

Taneisha scoffed and crossed her arms over her chest. "You think I have your mate? Why would I do that?"

Ray stepped in then, his voice gentle but firm. "Taneisha, that's not what Caden said," Ray said quietly, his tone admonishing. "We need to find Sera before anything else happens to her. Can you help us?"

Taneisha sighed heavily and uncrossed her arms, her expression softening slightly. "You can come in," she said after a moment of thought.

She gestured for us to come inside her now all too familiar demesne and motioned for Ray to follow as well. The tall oak spread overhead, the brook babbled along the far side of the glen, and the mossy couch all were unchanged from the last time we'd been here.

"So you admit you know where Sera is?" Franc pressed.

She shrugged, her gaze flitting between the three of us. "I might. I might not."

"We need to know," I said. "The Lowes have taken Marcos, Liam, and Emrys hostage. No doubt they'll come for Franc and I soon. If we're not able to produce Sera or point them in the right direction, we might have to recommend they seek you out next."

Taneisha listened intently and then nodded slowly. "I suppose I might know Sera's location. If I help you, what will you give me in return?" she asked with a sly smile.

Franc glanced at me before answering. At least we were on the right track. "What do you want?" he asked cautiously.

Taneisha shrugged nonchalantly and crossed her arms over her chest as she thought it over for a moment. My chest tightened as I wondered how long the fae would draw things out. Did she even know whether Sera was safe? But by now I knew better than to irritate the fae, so I held in my anxiety and my tongue.

Ray cleared his throat. "The last time we talked, Tany, I thought you'd said you were going to rethink your ways. I'm surprised you have since caused trouble for Sera."

"Ray!" Taneisha exclaimed, closing the distance between them. "How can you think that? Sera is my friend, and I would never place her in harm's way."

"Yet you concede you know where she is," Franc said. "Please, she could be in danger. You have to help us."

Taneisha gripped Ray's arm, shaking her head. "Sera's fine, I know it. She's in a very safe place."

"Sera's not fine. She called for us to come to her," I said.

Incongruously, Taneisha smiled like that was the best news ever, which it certainly wasn't. "I knew it! See, she's doing so well with her magic!"

I shared a look with Franc, who looked as lost as I felt.

Ray ran his fingers down Taneisha's bare arm. "Why don't you slow down and explain, dear?"

Taneisha sighed, her gaze flicking between the three of us, but mostly lingering on Ray's big, brown eyes. "I had a feeling that Sera was special, so I sent her on a quest for herself."

"We all know Sera is special," Franc replied. "But why another quest?"

The corner of Taneisha's lips curved up. "She's even more special than you suspect, demi-god. I knew if I could bring her to this realm, she would discover her true potential."

"So you kidnapped her?" Franc asked incredulously. "And took her to faery?"

"I didn't kidnap her!" Taneisha exclaimed, though she had the grace to look just a little guilty. "I merely opened the way and then set her on the path without consulting anyone else first. Sera needed to discover all that she's capable of with her magic. If what you say is true, that she was able to contact you, then I was right! She has already achieved so much in such a short amount of time!"

"Right? Sera's been getting a better handle on her magic with her mates help. Sure, she might get even better in faery, but at what cost?" I asked quietly. "Sera has been through hell with your quests and we've been worried sick about her safety. You have no idea how relieved I am to hear you know where she is, but I assure you we have reason to fear for Sera."

Taneisha furrowed her brows, and for once I thought I'd actually gotten her attention. "What do you mean, fear for her?"

It was Franc who answered. "Back at the Heart of the Desert temple Emrys and I stepped through a mirror into a future where Sera had died because we weren't there to protect her."

The blood ran out Taneisha's rosy cheeks. "She'll be safe in faery. She has to be."

"What if you're wrong?" Franc asked.

For once, Taneisha appeared humbled by the situation. I would have relished the moment if Sera's safety wasn't in question.

"I can understand your spontaneous and misguided attempt to help Sera," Ray replied. "But why send her to faery, a dangerous land for those not familiar with its ways?"

Taneisha nodded slowly before turning to Ray with an apologetic smile on her face. "I am sorry, but I can't reveal my reasons. Not yet. But we could check on her and make sure she's okay?"

Ray smiled softly and cupped Taneisha's cheek in his palm before leaning down and pressing a gentle kiss to her forehead. "That's my gal," he said softly before turning back to us with a determined glint in his eye. "Let's get Sera home."

Taneisha snapped her fingers, opening a portal within the glen.

Franc sighed. "Not another portal," he muttered.

The fae shrugged. "My home is just faery-adjacent, so it still takes a portal to get there."

We stepped through the portal and into a world completely removed from our own. I had never been to this faery before. This place was alive with magic and mystery. Every step we took was on a carpet of vibrant green grass, every breath inhaled the scent of a thousand wildflowers, and every glance revealed something new and wondrous.

Taneisha led us through the enchanted forest, her steps

confident, while we followed behind in awe. The trees here were massive and ancient, their branches thick with the passage of time. The leaves rustled in the wind with a sound like laughter, and it seemed as if the entire forest was alive with energy.

"I still remember that time you brought me here," Ray mused as he stared off into the treetops. "Maybe once we send Sera home with her mates we can linger a bit before heading back home?"

Taneisha bit her lip, blushing. "I am fond of lingering."

I spent a little too much time pondering how things might work between the tall, stocky minotaur and the diminutive fae. I blamed my incubus spirit and graphic imagination. As long as Franc and I left faery with Sera, I didn't care how long Ray and Taneisha stayed behind dallying.

The path we were following wound around tall stones that seemed to have been placed there by some unseen hand long ago. It eventually opened up into a large clearing, across from which a large stone castle loomed high above us like an imposing guardian of this magical realm. The air was heavy with anticipation as Taneisha led us closer to the castle's entrance.

"These are the lands of the Summer Court," Taneisha explained. "I sent Sera here."

"I thought you knew where Sera was?" I asked.

Taneisha shrugged. "More or less? She's in faery and wouldn't have passed anywhere without being noticed."

"Because she's a mage?" Franc asked.

"Because she's Sera," Taneisha said, winking.

We approached the gates where two guards watched our approach with apparent disinterest. The guards looked at us with a mixture of suspicion and curiosity. I could feel their eyes on me as if they were trying to figure out what I was and why I was there. Taneisha spoke up, asking if they had seen a human mage by the name of Sera Lowe.

The guards exchanged a look, then the one on the left stepped forward.

"We have seen her," he said, his voice low and gravelly. "She was here two days ago."

I stepped forward, my heart pounding in my chest. "Where is she now?"

"We don't know. She had unfortunate timing, I fear. The lady herself was ushering her to safety when the manticore attacked."

We all exchanged a glance, trying to make sense of what we'd just heard. A manticore?

"What happened?"

"I'm sorry to report it flew off with her."

He might as well have kicked me in the gut. "Where did it take her?" I asked, my voice tight with worry.

The guard shrugged. "It flew off toward the north," he said, gesturing helpfully. "We can't be sure where it went after that."

"And you just let it drag her off?" Franc demanded.

"There's no letting a manticore do anything, sir. It took down two of our own and we had others to protect. If you wish, we can take you to see Lady Alia, who surely can answer all of your questions. She's busy receiving other guests, but I'm sure she'll be happy to speak with you later."

"Thanks for your help," Ray replied, "but we can't spare the time right now." He pulled us away from the guards and the castle. "We can argue with them or we can go after Sera."

"We have to find her," Taneisha said, her voice determined and strong. "I won't rest until she is safe and sound back at home with her mates."

Ray pulled Taneisha into a big hug. "You know what, Tany? I'm proud of you."

"You are?" she asked, beaming up at him. "Really?"

He nodded, his big horns bouncing. "I am. I mean, you need to keep working on being more communicative and collaborative, but the way that you shifted gears and are working to help find Sera, this is real growth."

"Less growth. More finding the manticore," Franc ordered.

"It's all growth," Ray replied, with a knowing chuckle.

As we made our way through the forest, walking northward for nearly an hour, I couldn't help but feel a deep sense of foreboding. I glanced at my companions and could see they were feeling it too; their faces were grim and determined as they marched on in search of Sera. We had to find her before it was too late; there was no other option.

Suddenly, a loud roar echoed through the trees, and I felt a chill run down my spine. "What's the chance that's not the manticore?" I asked.

We all froze for a moment before breaking into a sprint towards the sound, not knowing what we would find when we arrived but knowing that whatever it was would be better than not finding Sera at all. We reached an area overgrown with bushes, and we had to slow down, checking behind every turn.

My heart was pounding in my chest as the four of us

cautiously edged closer to the source of the roar. We had no idea what we would find, but I suspected it wouldn't be good. We rounded a turn and suddenly the manticore was upon us. The enormous beast emerged from the shadows and I felt my blood run cold. The manticore's eyes blazed with rage and its claws outstretched as if ready to attack. It reared up on its hind legs, towering over us and roaring in anger. I felt my heart sink in my chest as I realized just how much trouble we were in.

"Run!" Ray shouted, pushing Taneisha ahead of him as he ran back the way we had come.

My feet moved of their own accord as I followed Ray, Franc and Taneisha running in front of me. But it was too late; the manticore had flown over us and now blocked our escape route with its massive body. It had trapped us.

"What do we do?" Franc asked, his voice full of anger.

I stepped forward, determined to face this beast head on if I had to. "I think it's time for a little negotiation," I said bravely. "Manticore, listen to me: We want Sera back and we're willing to do whatever it takes to get her back safely. If you let her go now, no one has to get hurt."

The manticore seemed to consider my words for a moment, but it didn't last long. It snarled and lunged at us, but Taneisha held it back with a powerful spell. I watched in awe as she spoke to the beast in a soothing voice, trying to calm it down enough that we could get some answers from it.

Taneisha stepped forward bravely, her hands glowing with magical energy. "Let's see if we can reason with him," she said calmly.

But the manticore was not interested in reason; it lunged forward and swiped at us with its claws. I jumped back, narrowly avoiding its attack. Ray stepped up and sent a blast of energy at the beast, which only made it angrier. The manticore roared in rage, its long claws slashing through the air as it charged us again. We all backed away, but it was too late. The beast had us pinned down between bushes and trees and there was nowhere to run.

DARKNESS RISING

SERA

The faery Vedreel looked around, as if checking for eavesdroppers. "Yes," he said in a hushed voice. "But it is forbidden for me to reveal his identity to you. You'll need to speak to your mother, or perhaps the Lady Alia would also know." He glanced back at me, then his eyes widened as I produced another glowing green orb in my palm and directed the two to spin around each other. "That is most impressive! I can't wait to see what else you can do with your power, Sera Lowe."

I felt such a sense of pride and accomplishment that I was tempted to crow about it to everyone I met. But I couldn't deny that there was also a part of me that was desperate to know my father's identity—and why neither my mother nor grandmother would tell me who he was? My missing father had been an open wound for most of my life; an unexplained absence that hung over every conversation my mother and I had like a dark cloud.

Now I knew why she had never told me who he was; he wasn't human! He was fae! The revelation raised even more questions than answers, but at least now I knew where to look.

I had been so focused on my little orbs of green magic that I hadn't noticed the fog rising around us, nor the rotting smell of dank swamp. There was a moment of silence as we both looked around, not sure what to make of things, but then Vedreel let out a low whistle.

"Uh-oh. I should have known better, encouraging you to work magic at this time of year, and so near the swamplands."

"What is it?" I asked him, unable to take my eyes away from the black tendrils now winding around our ankles.

"We have an unwelcome visitor," he replied.

Suddenly there was a loud boom. The dome of earth over us split open, but instead of daylight, a rolling black fog poured into the cavern.

I gasped as the fog swirled around us, and I could feel its icy tendrils reaching out to touch my skin. Vedreel stepped in front of me protectively, but it was too late— something else, something deadly, was already here.

A behemoth emerged from the fog, a giant hulking mass of blackness with glowing red eyes and razor-sharp claws, so dark I couldn't entirely make out its form. It hissed and growled as it advanced on us, wrapped within shadows as it moved forward, its powerful tail lashing the air. I took a step back in shock, but Vedreel stood his ground, summoning up a magical shield to protect us both.

The creature roared in anger and lashed out with its claws, but the shield deflected them. It tried again and again to break through Vedreel's barrier but failed each time. Finally it stopped attacking, seeming to realize that it couldn't break through the magical barrier no matter how hard it tried. Instead, it shifted its gaze towards me—and growled.

Vedreel turned towards me and said softly: "The darkness feeds on fae magic, but it appears especially drawn to the unique flavor of your magic. My barrier won't hold for long. We must flee now while we still can."

Without another word he grabbed my hand and pulled me away from the creature, sprinting down the hall toward the exit. We rounded a corner and suddenly there was a loud crash behind us. The creature had broken through Vedreel's barrier and was now in pursuit of us. Vedreel and I ran as fast as we could, but the creature was relentless. Its claws scraped against the walls, echoing through the cave like thunder. I could feel its presence behind us like a malevolent force, pushing us ever forward. We ran faster, but still it followed close behind, wisps of shadows licking at our heels.

I was out of breath and my legs ached from running, but I knew I had to fight if I wanted to survive. Taking a deep breath, I reached for the depths of my power and conjured a fireball in my hands. I threw it at the creature, watching as it exploded against its hide and sent it reeling back.

The creature let out an angry roar and charged back towards us, claws raised. Without thinking, I conjured another fireball and threw it at the creature again. This time it didn't recoil—it kept coming!

Vedreel grabbed my arm and pulled me behind him as he created a magical barrier around us both. The shadow beast kept advancing, claws slashing through Vedreel's barrier like paper.

The beast of darkness advanced on us, its red eyes blazing with hatred. Vedreel held his arms outstretched and a magical barrier glowed around us both. The beast lunged forward, claws slashing through the barrier like paper. Vedreel summoned another barrier just in time to keep us safe, but I sensed this one wouldn't last long either.

Vedreel gritted his teeth and focused all his energy into the shield, but it was no use—the beast seemed determined to break through. I could see the strain on Vedreel's face as he fought to keep the shield up, and I knew he wouldn't be able to hold it for much longer. I watched as the beast of darkness attacked Vedreel, clawing at his magical barrier with a ferocity that was terrifying to behold.

Vedreel fought bravely, summoning up more and more magical barriers to protect us both, but it was no use. We didn't have time to escape the rest of the way up the cave to the surface and defend against the beast at the same time. The beast seemed determined to break through and I could see the strain on Vedreel's face as he fought to keep the shield up.

And then it happened. Vedreel stumbled backwards and his barrier flickered out of existence. I screamed in terror as the beast advanced on him, and I knew there was nothing I could do but watch in horror as it sunk his razor-like claws deep into Vedreel's chest.

But then something amazing happened—by instinct a burst of light appeared from nowhere, bathing the entire room in a brilliant white glow. It seemed to come from me! This time I didn't hesitate—I summoned up all my strength and threw out my hands towards the creature, releasing a powerful wave of magic that sent it flying back into the shadows from whence it came.

The beast hissed and roared as it tried to break through my magical light barrier, its claws slashing at the air. I shivered in fear, but I kept my focus and continued to channel my magic. The beast seemed determined to get through and I could feel its rage emanating from it like a physical force.

It exhausted me to expend so much energy, but I didn't give up. With every ounce of strength I had left, I maintained the barrier between us, keeping the beast at bay.

Still on the floor, Vedreel groaned and coughed before spitting up a dark gray blood. I had no idea how mortal a wound he'd suffered considering the type of fae he was, but I knew I needed to get him to a healer. Fast.

"Any ideas for how to shake this beast and get the hells out of here?" I asked.

Vedreel's face was pale and his breathing labored, but he cracked a weak smile. "There is a way out of here," he said, his voice barely more than a whisper. "A portal, but I'm not strong enough to open one, but it's a talent all fae possess."

I looked at him in confusion. His reminder of my fae heritage was still a shock. "I can do portals?"

He nodded his head slowly. "You should be able to, but you must trust your powers. It's our only chance at escaping this beast. If you can open the portal, we might slip through and make our escape."

My mind raced as I considered our options. Could I really open a portal? I had no idea how—and even if I could, would it be safe? The beast was still clawing at my glowing barrier between us, determined to break through and finish us. It seemed like an impossible task—but what other choice did I have? I wouldn't be able to hold the light barrier forever.

Finally, I made up my mind. Taking a deep breath, I reached for my magic and focused on the task ahead of me. This time when my magic flared up around me, it felt different—stronger and more powerful than ever before. I envisioned all the places I'd visited in faery so far, trying to pick one that would be the best destination, but I couldn't quite decide. The air shimmered as a portal opened behind us, revealing a swirling vortex of light beyond its opening. I couldn't quite make out what was on the other side, but I knew the beast was on this side, so it wasn't much of a contest.

The portal was unstable, flickering in and out of existence, but it was our only way out. I could feel my protective barrier beginning to falter, so I knew we had to act fast. Vedreel groaned in pain as I hoisted him to his feet and we stumbled towards the portal. He could barely stand and I had no idea if he would make it—but there was no time to worry about that now. We had to get away from the beast before it broke through my barrier and killed us both.

We reached the portal just as my magical barrier vanished completely and the beast let out a roar of triumph. We stepped through the portal just as it began to close—the swirling vortex of light sputtering around us. The beast bounded toward us, all black claws, teeth, and pointy tail wrapped in darkness. I gathered my energy and threw out one more blast to prevent it from following us into the portal.

"No!" Vedreel exclaimed. "Not while in the portal!"

But Vedreel's warning came too late. My magic was already spent, setting off a cascade reaction between the portal, the remnants of the barrier, and my parting blast towards the dark beast. An explosion rang through my ears as a blast of hot air threw us to the ground. Clods of dirt rained down on us, blocking out the light and air as the world faded into blackness.

TWO BEASTS

FRANC

I watched in horror as the manticore attacked us with its sharp claws. I could feel my heart pounding in my chest as I prepared to fight back. Drawing upon my magic, I called forth the wild energy of the forest to my aid but did not expect that I would draw any response. To my surprise, the grass and bushes around me stirred and a deep groan echoed through the trees.

Suddenly, all manner of birds, squirrels, and mice erupted from their hiding places but also fantastical fae creatures emerged from everywhere—even some glowing, floating balls of light spun around us, weightless. Yet the birds weren't familiar, and neither were the other beasts. These had colors I'd never seen before or even dreamed of. And the squirrels and rabbits had massive teeth. But what had I been expecting, summoning within a faery forest? These weren't the dryads and nymphs I'd find at home. No, these were their fae counterparts, and they'd come ready to kick ass.

The manticore paused momentarily when faced with a resistance it didn't expect but soon overcame its confusion and roared at us threateningly when the ground beneath us once again trembled. We froze for a moment before the manticore advanced on us once more. The trees groaned loudly, their roots twisted in distress as vines and branches swayed wildly, as if they were moving of their own accord. The wind blew erratically and leaves flew into our faces as we tried to avoid the beast's snapping jaws.

What was going on under us? Was the forest itself in revolt, or was this just a normal day in faery?

A loud boom echoed through the trees, and I felt a chill run down my spine. The earth beneath us buckled and heaved. I sensed the tang of magic in the air and looked to find my suspicion mirrored in the eyes of my companions.

"What's going on?" Ray shouted as he looked around for an explanation.

"Something's happening underneath us. Powerful forces are at play here," Taneisha said.

The ground beneath us suddenly quaked and then erupted open, sending us tumbling into the darkness below. I hit the ground hard, my breath knocked out of me as the shock of the fall set in. Ray, Caden, and Taneisha sprawled out beside me, their faces contorted in pain.

The manticore roared above us, its giant claws reaching down into the cave as it tried to grab hold of us. We scrambled to our feet backed away from the opening above into the cave, our only hope being that we could lose it in the pitch-black. But instead of getting darker, a soft light filled the room, and the air crackled with magic. The magic had a familiar tang, but where was it coming from? The earth itself?

"I smell Sera in the air," Caden said. "She can't be far."

"We'll find her," I replied.

But then an oppressive aura of dark magic swept over us. Separate from the manticore above us, I could feel a new dangerous presence before I even saw it. I sensed that whatever creature lurked in this cave was out of place, even for faery.

A giant black creature with glowing red eyes and razor-sharp teeth and claws emerged from the shadows. Its blackened fur shimmered in the dim light, and its howl echoed off the walls of the cave like thunder. It was a creature that belonged in nightmares, not reality. But I stood my ground, determined not to let fear take over me. The beast snarled at me as if it could sense my courage, but I refused to back down. This was my fight now.

"As if one deadly beast wasn't enough," I muttered, looking around for anything that might help us fend off the beast. Instead, it just stared at me with those eerie glowing eyes as if trying to decide what to make of me before finally turning its head away from mine in irritation or disappointment—I couldn't tell which—and then walked away from us as if we were unimportant pieces on a chessboard that had been swept aside by an invisible hand. Instead, its attention went to the mound of dirt at the far end of the cave.

When it began digging, Taneisha pulled us into a huddle. "I can't fight the darkness, it feeds on fae magic. Anything I throw at it will only strengthen it."

"The darkness? That's its name?" I asked.

Taneisha nodded. "I'll send up a beacon for aid. Since it won't be aimed at the darkness, it won't be able to feed off of it. Hopefully, some are nearby and my call will summon forth some help from faery for our fight against the darkness." Taneisha closed her eyes for a moment as she moved her fingers in an intricate pattern, focusing her energy. The fae lifted her hand toward the sky and a flare shot up from her hand like a giant sparkling firework, shooting red and orange sparks in its wake.

I stepped forward, my eyes widening as the mound began to shift and heave.

"What's it doing?" Ray asked, his voice full of awe. "It's like it's alive."

Taneisha shook her head slowly. "I don't know, but it is clearly not a natural thing."

The creature dug deep enough that a bright light burst through the dirt. It yelped and stopped digging, backing away from the mound, which was now glowing brighter than ever before. The light seemed to beckon me closer, and despite my fear of the beast I found myself compelled to step forward.

My heart raced as I watched the beast pick a new angle and resume digging into the mound of dirt. I didn't know what was underneath, but whatever it was, it seemed to be alive and emanating a powerful magic. A magic the beast craved.

"We have to do something before it reaches whatever is inside," I said. "Something, or someone, is under there," I said. I shared a quick look with Caden, and I saw my concern returned in his red-tinged gaze. I didn't understand why, but I feared Sera was under there, and I knew he worried the same. "It's Sera. It's got to be."

Caden swore under his breath and stepped forward, his eyes narrowing in determination. "I say we take the fight to it. It's our only chance at saving Sera."

I swallowed hard and nodded my agreement before turning back towards the beast that was still digging away at the mound of dirt like an excavator on steroids. As if sensing our presence, it paused for a moment and looked up at us with those glowing red eyes before continuing its work without fear of our presence. That's when I realized this creature wasn't just some mindless beast—it knew exactly what it was doing and why we were here.

"Taneisha, can you push back the dirt?" I asked.

"Now that, I can do," she said with a decisive nod. "But it'll draw the beast's attention."

Ray stepped between Taneisha and the darkness, willing to use his massive frame to protect her. "I'll hold off the beast."

Taneisha gasped, and I swore her eyes glistened with unshed tears over Ray's show of valor. She recovered a moment later, focusing on the task and waving her hands again in an intricate pattern toward the mound as Taneisha began chanting quietly under her breath. The dirt magically swept away from the top of the mound, pile after pile pushed to the side.

As the light in the room intensified, it was as if someone had turned a spotlight on. All eyes were drawn to the mound in the center of the cave. The light grew brighter and brighter until finally, a beam of light shot up from within the pile of dirt, illuminating the cave like daylight.

The beast let out a howl of pain, as if the light had burned it. It scurried away from the mound and into the shadows, disappearing without a trace.

The light continued to grow until a spiderweb-like dome of light became visible as the dirt shifted and cleared, revealing two figures within. Freed of the weight of the dirt, one figure stood up and the web of light dissipated, revealing our mate.

"Sera!"

We flew towards her, Caden and I. Our arms seemed to move of their own accord and wrapped tightly around her. We could feel an electric surge of joy as the warmth of her hugged us back - our missing mate was reunited and safe with us again.

"It's okay now," Caden whispered softly, running his hand over her hair to soothe her. "You're not alone. We're here for you now, and we're not going anywhere."

"I think you can safely say you won't be going anywhere without one of us maybe ever again," I growled into her ear.

"That's my alphas," she murmured, hugging us back. "I missed you guys too," she said, pulling away from us all too soon. "I'm worn out from fending off the beast and keeping up that air pocket. Can you help me pull Vedreel clear?" It was only then that I noticed the unconscious fae lying at her feet, because whoever it was, was almost completely covered in dirt.

I didn't know who Vedreel was, other than someone Sera had been protecting from the darkness beast. I couldn't help feeling a sense of gratitude and admiration for this brave, selfless woman who had risked everything to save a stranger.

"Hey Taneisha, can you dig him out?" Caden asked.

Taneisha stepped closer, and with a few swipes of her fingers, the rest of the dirt sloughed away. Sera bent over the wrinkled and weathered fae who might have been half willow tree, checking his pulse and forehead. She sighed in relief at what she found, so the old guy must have survived the ordeal after all.

Sera stood back up and looked between Ray and Taneisha, and smiled my way. "Not that I'm complaining, but how did you convince Taneisha to help you?"

Ray winked and nudged my shoulder. "Your mates asked me for help, so I helped them find Taneisha. She knows how important you are to your mates, so of course she wanted you safe and happy with them again."

Sera pursed her lips, clearly doubting Ray's version of events.

Taneisha shrugged. "I never could say no to Ray, and Franc and Caden just looked so awfully worried for you. They didn't believe that I brought you to faery as a favor. Can you imagine?"

Sera shook her head. "Yeah, T, I can believe it. Remind me to thank you for that knock upside the head later." I wondered what she meant, but then Sera looked at each of us with that brilliant smile of hers, looking more relieved than I'd ever seen her, and all other questions fled my thoughts.

Sera took in a deep breath and said, "Thank you all for coming after me. Now let's get Vedreel out of here before the beast returns."

Ray stepped up and easily scooped the elder fae into his arms. Taneisha flicked her fingers in the air toward the sky, materializing a set of steps out of packed dirt up to the grass and open sky above. The four of us then hurried up the stairs and out of the cave, eager to put some distance between us and the razor-clawed beast.

When we reached the surface, the foe we encountered was one I had been preparing to face for some time, however, this was not how I had envisioned our first meeting. I had hoped for more favorable odds, yet here we were.

A LOWE RECKONING

SERA

I climbed to the surface, my body aching with every step, informing me not so quietly just all the places I'd decorated with various bruises. Caden took the lead up the stairs while Franc hadn't left my side, guiding my every step like I was some sort of fragile princess. The Sera from a couple of weeks ago would have brushed him off, independent to the core. But with those puppy dog eyes and the reassuring touch of his fingers against my spine, I gave over and leaned close to him, reveling in the heat of him against me.

When we reached the top, it took my brain a couple of moments to process the scene before us. We were surrounded in the best and worst possible ways. In the realm of best, my heart sang as I laid my eyes on a very disgruntled and exhausted Emrys, Liam, and Marcos. It hadn't been that long since I'd seen them, but I couldn't deny the sense of relief having all five of my mates with me.

On the flip side, my grams stood surrounded by her

usual retinue at the top of the stairs with a notable plus one: the Lady Alia. A pair of mercenary mages and a handful of fae guards flanked them both, their attention shifting back and forth between all of us, alert for danger. Gram's gaze ran over us, her look of barely managed disdain directed at either the condition of our clothes, the gaping maw of the cave, Taneisha for so many reasons, or the unconscious fae in Ray's arms.

I refused to consider that she might be directing that look of profound disdain at my five mates. They were mine, and Grams would just have to suck it up and accept them.

I hadn't seen Grams for almost a year, but she looked just as regal and ageless as ever. She'd pulled her salt and pepper hair back into a tight bun and she wore a green blazer over a black pencil skirt and burgundy blouse, the colors used in the distinctive sigil of House Lowe. She stood ramrod straight with her hands on her hips in her classic 'the matriarch has arrived' pose. I'd bet money one of her perfectly manicured nails had an emerald or sapphire on it from that extensive collection she loved to show off.

Grams closed the distance between us, her gaze running over me in a way that was both loving and assessing. My heart swelled with a mixture of happiness and love but also dread as I silently prayed she wasn't about to lecture me. To my surprise, Grams held out her arms when we were close enough together for the gesture, drawing me into an affectionate hug despite me being filthy with cave dirt and smelling of fae magic, and no doubt blood from the beast's claws digging into my shoulder blade. Grams stepped back again, and I saw in her eyes what words couldn't express - relief at seeing me alive.

"Seraphina Lowe! You had me worried sick! We've been searching everywhere for you, even dragging this ragtag group here into faery! We had to summon all our combined strength to chase off a nasty beast lurking around the hole you just sauntered out of. You do not know how happy I am to see you safe again! Now, let's get you home where you belong before it returns!" she said, squeezing me tight against her bosom. "I'm sure an extended stay at the manor will do you a world of good after this ordeal."

I pulled away gently but firmly. Although her offer to stay at House Lowe was kind, my plans were with my mates. When Emrys, Liam, and Marcos continued to hang back, I instantly suspected grams had the mages limiting their movement, which I wasn't about to tolerate.

"Thank you for the offer, Grams. I can't believe you found me out here but I'm glad you did."

"Your friends," she waved at Emrys, Liam, and Marcos, "insisted that you were in faery. I went straight to my friend Lady Alia, who informed me a manticore had flown off with you. What else could we do but charge off into the wilds after you?"

"Not to interrupt this reunion," Ray said, interrupting us. "But we need to get this fae to a healer."

I turned to Emrys. "Em, can you take a look at Vedreel?" I gestured to Ray, who rushed to Emrys and laid Vedreel on the ground between them.

Emrys bent over the elder fae and placed a hand on his chest and another across his forehead. "What happened to him?"

"I happened," I replied. "I tried to fireball while inside my portal and it caused an enormous shock wave. The roof caved in on us, and while I created an air pocket to protect us, I'm pretty sure Vedreel hit his head."

I circled around Vedreel and pulled Liam and then Marcos into soul-soothing hugs. From the way they inhaled my scent and growled as they held me right, I knew each of them would need a lot more cuddly skin time before their beasts would let me out of their sight again.

"Wait, what were you throwing a fireball at?" Marcos asked.

"A darkness beast," I explained, pulling away from Marcos. "How is he?" I asked Emrys.

"He's growing stronger," Emrys replied, his attention fully on the fae except for a moment when he flashed that devastating, cocky smile of his up at me. "I'd wager he'll wake up at any moment."

Lady Alia stepped forward, her keen eyes widening. "Where is the beast of darkness now?"

"I was under a pile of dirt and didn't see," I said, looking to Franc, Caden, and Taneisha for an explanation.

Franc cleared his throat. "We fought to hold it off, but the beast ran when you did that spiderweb of light thing."

"Oh wow, I'm surprised that actually worked," I replied, earning me a wry smile from Franc.

"Did you see where it went?" Lady Alia asked Franc.

He nodded. "The beast ran further down into the cave complex."

Lady Alia's face twisted with anger and determination. "Then we must go after it," Lady Alia said, motioning to her guards, who rushed forward to her side. "The longer we leave it unchecked, the more dangerous it will become. Titus, head back to the Summer Court and bring back reinforcements."

Titus gave a quick nod. "At once, my lady." He turned, cast a portal, and swept through it.

Emrys helped a revived and re-energized-looking Vedreel to his feet, helping him shake off the dirt and muck covering his long robes. The elder waved him off, unconcerned with the state of his clothes.

"I'll come with you, Lady Alia," Vedreel said. "My knowledge of the caves below will aid your cause."

The lady inclined her head his way. "If you feel up for it, we would be grateful for your direction."

A shadow passed over us followed by a deafening roar. The guards were on instant alert, weapons in hand, while Lady Alia and Grams both threw magical shields overhead, layers of ruby and gossamer filtering the light.

"Miriss!" Vedreel shouted. "Stand down, fair folk. The beast is with me."

Grams gaped at the elder fae. "But it's a manticore!"

Vedreel dragged a hand over his gnarled features. "Truly, madam, but Miriss is my eldest friend. I beg you relent."

Lady Alia and Grams shared a look and a shrug, then dropped their shields. The guards were not so easily swayed, remaining vigilant with their weapons.

The manticore landed a moment later, bounded over to Vedreel, and licked his face with his enormous tongue. Vedreel laughed and laughed while the rest of us gave the two some room.

"Wait a second," Taneisha spoke up, eyes alit with

burning excitement. "Did you just say, my portal?" she asked me.

Everyone's glanced at me at the same time and I felt the smile curling the corners of my mouth. My gaze flicked to Grams, who'd arched her brow at Taneisha's question. Just how much did Grams know, or suspect, about my powers? Did she know who my father was? Mom had been absent so much of my life, but surely Grams had known the truth from her.

My mates all exchanged glances, but it was Caden who spoke. "It appears so, Taneisha," he said with an irresistible smile. "If it weren't for Sera's quick thinking and powerful magic, who knows what might have happened to us in there with that beast."

I shook my head and waved them off. "Let's not get too dramatic. It was just one little spiderweb. And a fireball. And a portal."

Lady Alia nodded in agreement. "You have the courage and power of a warrior, Sera. You should be proud, Ms. Lowe."

Grams pursed her lips, and I knew that fire dancing in her eyes was evidence of her plans for my future. "I've always been proud of my granddaughter. Now, it appears she's a force few could reckon with."

I couldn't help but let out a rueful laugh. "You expected something like this would happen when you sent me here, didn't you?" I asked Taneisha.

Taneisha let out a tinkling giggle, joyfully spinning on her toes in a slow circle. "Of course, I did." Her voice was light and filled with triumph. "I knew your magic was different, and I suspected I knew the reason. You just needed the opportunity, time, and the right surroundings to blossom, so off to faery I sent you. You have certainly proved me right."

I shook my head at her. I didn't appreciate her methods, but I had to hand it to the fickle fae. She'd been right. I didn't know how Taneisha had figured out my heritage or the peculiarities of my gifts, but I was grateful to know I was part fae and to have those powers opened to me at last.

"You freely admit you abducted my granddaughter?" Grams asked, her voice deceptively sweet.

Taneisha stopped spinning, her attention fixed entirely Grams. "Yes. Well, at least this one time. The time with all of them before wasn't an abduction because Sera went willingly. And I will not apologize, not for any of it. I felt it was necessary to bring her to faery so she'd find her way," Taneisha rattled on. She straightened her shoulders and tossed back her head, determination glowing in her eyes. "I suspect you know why."

I'd become unaccustomed to anyone else daring my Gram's temper, and I found it refreshing to have someone other than me calling Ms. Dara Lowe's bluff.

Grams frowned, sparing a glance my way, but then simply sighed. "Yes, I suppose I do."

Taneisha nodded. "Indeed. Your granddaughter is extremely powerful. Lady Alia, if I may, the Summer Court would be wise to acknowledge her heritage."

Lady Alia's grave attention turned to me. "Do you seek to claim a place at court?"

"Woah," I held up my hands. I wasn't even used to spending time around the supe community, and I imagined the fae courts to be about a zillion times more political. No! No, thank you! "Respectfully, Lady Alia, I need some time to process these revelations."

"That's some wisdom, child. If you change your mind, you know where to find us," Alia replied, then turned to Vedreel. "Now, let's go see what other surprises this cave has in store for us." She then motioned to her guards. "Come, we have a beast to manage."

"My beast and I would love to assist," Vedreel replied, bending deep at the waist towards Lady Alia.

Miriss whined, but Vedreel tsked. "Now, now, Miriss. It's just a little dark."

By Miriss's frown, I assumed she didn't agree, yet she followed Vedreel all the same.

The fae headed down into the cave and I was glad to not be going with them this time. I looked around at my mates, who'd been conspicuously quiet, and something clicked. "Speaking of abductions... Grams, are my guys here with you to help you find me, or did you abduct them?"

Grams took a long breath in and then paused. "Can't it be both?"

"This seems like a private family matter," Ray said, deftly interrupting us. He held out his hand to Taneisha, and she practically leapt into his arms. "Shall we take our leave?" he murmured to her.

Taneisha flicked her fingers and summoned a portal, pulling Ray along behind her. I thought I spied The Chillax Center through the surface.

"Peace out, supes. Catch you later!"

"I wish you all well," Ray added, their portal winking out a moment later.

Franc ran his hand through his hair. "Always going for the dramatic exit."

I chuckled, but then remembered why Taneisha and Ray had scampered away so quickly, and turned my focus back to Grams.

"Grams, what were you thinking?" I crossed my arms. "You can't just force my guys to do your bidding."

"We wanted to come," Emrys said, but I raised a palm to cut him off, silently communicating that this was a conversation between me and my grams.

Gram's expression softened, and she looked at me with understanding. "Oh, little one. I understand why you are upset. I wanted to protect you and keep you safe. I certainly never imagined that I would be capable of taking such drastic measures."

To their credit, Gram's guards didn't laugh or smile, but one of them, I thought his name was Erebus, did arch a brow her way.

"Never imagined?" I repeated back to her, my tone mocking. I sighed. I was still angry, but I also understood where Grams was coming from. She had done what she felt she had to do to protect me, and my mates were all safe, so perhaps I owed her a pass this time?

"Fine. I forgive you, Grams. But please, no more secrets. Okay?"

Grams nodded. "You are right, granddaughter. I should have been more honest with you about your heritage. I apologize for that. But I also believe it was a necessary risk. We never knew what, if anything, would surface from your birthright."

I sighed. I was still frustrated, but I also understood

where Grams was coming from. She had done what she felt she had to do to protect me.

"I might not agree with your choice, but I can understand it."

Grams nodded. "No more secrets, I promise." Grams looked at my guys, one at a time, before her gaze narrowed on me again. "It seems like I'm not the only one keeping secrets today. Anything I should know about what happened between all of you on your fae-bound quests?" she asked me.

Not my guys. Me. I knew what she was asking.

"While winning back their legacies, the fates marked us as mates."

"All of you?"

"Uh huh."

"Oh, my," Grams drawled, looking at each of my guys again, as if appraising them for their future familial worth. "Well, it looks like I have some catching up to do. I'm sure you'll all explain everything to me in due time."

My guys nodded, and I smiled, relieved that Grams was taking this news much better than I thought she would.

"Thank you for understanding, Grams," I said.

Grams smiled, her eyes twinkling. "Who am I to argue with fate? Boys, welcome to the family. I trust you'll treat my granddaughter like the crown jewel she is." Grams motioned for her guards, but continued speaking to me. "Let's go back home. I have a special gift for you that's been a long time coming."

And with that, I summoned a portal and all of us disappeared through it, heading back to Grams' manor.

THERE'S NO PLACE LIKE HOME

I'd only been asleep in my new bed for a few hours, but I woke up refreshed and invigorated, eager to fully explore our new home. After demanding all five of my mates swear oaths of loyalty to the Lowe family line, my beaming grandmother had ushered us off to the gift she'd mentioned: our own house. The house, or maybe I should call it an estate, was one of the family properties in what was known unofficially as the mage section of town.

Exploring was easier said than done, considering Liam and Marcos had sandwiched me between their dozing selves. Last night, my mates had been solely focused on exploring me, not our newly gifted residence. It was so amazing to have this opportunity with my fated mates, and I'd never have imagined it, but I couldn't be happier with the situation. Or the men. I had a moment of pause, thinking back over these past few weeks, and it was still hard to believe I'd been abducted by the fae Taneisha, taken on a series of quests, and then found my fated mates in the supernova of hotness from my Goldenbriar Academy days.

It was all too much to take in.

But while that was running through my head, my body had other ideas. I felt a hand on my thigh, sliding up under my pajama shorts. The calloused pad of a finger traced along my folds and slid across my clit. My eyes popped open as I gasped for breath. Marcos was leaning over me, his dark eyes full of hunger as he leaned down to kiss me. His lips were soft at first, but then he pressed against mine more firmly and his tongue slid between them into my mouth.

I wrapped my arms around his neck and pulled him close against me as our tongues danced together in an erotic dance of their own. Marcos moved his hand from between my legs to around the small of my back. He pulled me against him as we lay on our sides facing each other. His kiss was an awakening of my body, and the heat between my thighs was immediate. I ran my palms down Marcos's back, feeling the contours of his muscles. He broke our kiss, pulling back to look at me.

"I'm not sure if you're ready for more after last night, but I need you so bad it hurts," Marcos whispered.

I knew my absence while I'd been in faery learning about my powers had hit my shifters the hardest. Their animalistic need to see me and reassure their beasts that their mate was safe and sound meant being apart from me had been a source of almost physical pain.

I leaned forward, nipping at his earlobe and whispering back, "I'm a faery-mage. I can handle anything you throw at me."

Marcos chuckled. "That's what I'm counting on."

Liam slid into place behind me, wrapping his arms around my waist as he nuzzled against my neck with soft kisses that made me shiver with anticipation of what was to come next. His hand slid up under my shirt, caressing my rib cage and stomach before finding its way up to cup one breast while he pinched the other nipple.

"Oh, gods!" My breathy voice betrayed how turned on I already was from Marcos' tender ministrations. The heat from his body seeped into mine through our skin-to-skin contact, warming every inch of flesh where we touched each other up to a fever pitch.

"You're so beautiful," Liam said against my earlobe before nibbling on it gently with his teeth before sucking it into his mouth for a moment.

I felt the bed shift behind me as Liam moved around. I had a moment to wonder what he was doing, but then I didn't care, because his hands were on my hips and his lips on my neck. I let out a shuddering breath as he nibbled along the sensitive skin of my neck and earlobe, sending shivers of anticipation down my spine.

"You feel so good in my arms," Liam murmured against my ear. "We should stay like this all day."

I turned within his embrace to face him, sliding one hand up into his hair at the nape of his neck while the other traced along the rippling muscles of his arms. "I'm not going to stay in bed all day," I said. "Aren't you curious about our new home?"

"I am," Marcos purred. "But first I'd love to watch you subdue a pair of beasts who are determined to devour you."

I was never one to back down from a challenge, and Marcos knew it. "I'd like to see them try."

Liam's eyes widened slightly with surprise, but then he smiled and nodded, turning me back towards Marcos and then moving behind me, pulling off our pajamas until we were all naked together. It was such a profoundly intimate moment that I had to stop for a moment to take it all in and appreciate it for what it meant: We'd found each other, fate had brought us together, the quests were in our rearview mirror, and now we were free to explore our new relationship together.

I ran my palms along Marcos' chest as he leaned forward against me again, peppering kisses down over my shoulder while he slid two fingers inside of me. He made sure not to push them in too far or move them too fast; instead he focused on rubbing across that sweet spot deep within me that made every nerve ending sizzle with pleasure. His thumb circled around my clit as he worked me with those skilled fingers until I was panting for breath under him.

"You're ready for more," Marcos said with a smile against the skin of my neck before biting down on it gently. "So am I."

Liam's love bites caught the chain around my neck which held the birth control charm Franc had gifted me. "I see Ms. Lowe wasn't able to talk you out of this necklace."

"Oh, hell no. It's staying on for now," I replied, panting under their touch. Grams had noticed the charm and quickly perceived its purpose, which hadn't surprised me for a mage of her caliber. "Grams can wait for her grandbabies, but I can't wait any longer for you."

I felt Marcos' erection sliding against my thigh, and I spread my legs to welcome him forward. He slid the tip of his cock through my wet folds, teasing me. I arched my back and cried out as he thrust into me, sliding in deep all the way to his hilt. My hands dug into his shoulders, holding onto him for dear life as he began thrusting in and out of me.

Liam's hands gripped my hips, holding me steady while he moved up behind me. He nuzzled against the back of my neck, then kissed a path down over one shoulder blade before nibbling on the other one. A moment later, I felt the head of his cock pressing against my ass, seeking entry.

I braced myself against Marcos' shoulders as Liam slid inside of me with a slow steady thrust forward that filled me up completely. There was a moment of discomfort at having both their cocks in such intimate contact within me at once, but it passed quickly as they began moving together in sync with each other.

"Oh gods! This is heaven!" I cried out between panting breaths. "You feel so good!" The feeling of being stretched full by them both was almost overwhelming, but never enough to make me want them to stop or slow down their pace even for a moment. Liam ran his calloused hand along my hip and up around to cup a breast while Marcos ran his fingertips along the sensitive flesh of my left arm while he held onto me with his other hand resting on the small of my back under Liam's supporting arm. As they moved within me together, every nerve ending in my body sizzling with pleasure from their touch and how perfectly they fit together.

Marcos and Liam were both holding me up now, their thrusts never losing momentum as they rocked against me. "Don't hold back," Marcos growled out against the side of neck as he nibbled on it again with those wicked cat-like fangs just barely breaking skin each time he did so.

His words sent an electric current through every nerve ending in my body. I felt the familiar tingle of my magic within my fingertips, and I knew the energy was building around us. I reached out with my mage energy, directing it into Marcos and Liam, blurring the lines separating us. Marcos' eyes widened with surprise as he felt my magic within him. He grinned at me as his fangs dropped, and then he bit down on my shoulder blade again, this time drawing blood. Liam's wolfish growl against my neck was followed by his bite, sending a fresh a wave of pleasure rolling over me.

The orgasm that hit then was unlike anything else I could have imagined. As we all came together, the room lit up with our combined magic's glow like a beacon in the night sky. A moment later, we all collapsed onto the bed in a heap, panting for breath in one another's arms.

"That... was..." Marcos panted out between breaths as he held us close to him while he recovered.

"Yeah," Liam replied with a satisfied smile on his face as he nuzzled against me and planted another kiss on my neck while still holding onto me tight like he'd die if he let go.

"Uh huh," I replied to them both with a smile of my own. We laid contentedly for a few minutes, but then I pulled myself up. This time, neither of them fought to keep me there.

"You're actually serious about exploring?" Liam asked, his voice sleepy again.

"I am," I said. I looked around the expansive bedroom and found a cream-colored silk robe thrown over one of the overstuffed lounge chairs bracketing the fireplace. I pulled it around myself, vaguely remembering finding it in the closet here last night. I stuffed my toes into a pair of matching slippers and then headed to the door.

Marcos pulled himself up onto one elbow. "You want company?"

"Nah, you guys get some rest. You've earned it," I said, seeing my smile returned in Marcos' eyes.

"I don't like you wandering around this estate in the wee hours of the morning," Liam said.

"Don't worry, I'm not leaving. I've got three other mates out there, a top of the line magical alarm system, plus the security detail Grams assigned us. For once, we can breathe easy."

"Okay, okay, we get it. Call if you need us," Marcos replied, tapping his forehead.

I headed out the door into the hallway and ran straight into an irate-looking Franc.

"What's wrong?" I started, but he cut me off.

Franc leaned in close to me, and I could feel the heat of his body as he got close enough for me to catch a whiff of his scent. He smelled of wild forest and wood smoke. He pulled me close, pinning me against him. The charge in the air between us was a little more feral than before, and it had an effect on me that was almost immediate.

Franc didn't seem to notice my body's reaction as he whispered into my ear. "Follow me." His husky words sent shivers of desire down my spine and straight into my belly, making me squirm against him for a moment before pulling away from him. Franc reached out and grabbed my hand, pulling me along behind him as he walked us down the hall. Franc stopped a few doors down, pulling it open and leading me inside behind him like a pet on a leash.

Franc led me into the room, the door clicking shut behind us. Franc turned to face me. The space was enormous, dominated by a massive bed with black sheets and a canopy with sheer curtains pulled back along each side and a black leather bench at the foot of the bed.

"It's time I deliver on that lesson I promised you back in that faery library." Franc's voice was firm, but not angry. There was something else there, almost like hunger. I felt it in my belly and between my legs in response to his commanding tone. "I'm going to spank you for putting yourself in danger. Multiple times." He walked up to me and circled me as he spoke, his words spinning around me like a web of control that I wanted him to wrap around me and hold there. "Tell me why you're being punished."

There was an edge of command in his voice that made my body respond with an almost automatic reply. "Because I recklessly ran headlong into danger to win back my mates legacies at their explicit request?"

He spun around again, stopping behind me again and leaning over so his lips were at my ear again, but this time he spoke softly instead of commanding or demanding answers from me. "Funny girl." Franc said as he untied the sash on my robe and sliding it off my shoulders and down my arms before letting it fall onto the floor at our feet. The heat from his breath against my ear sent shivers down my spine as he continued speaking. "That beast in the cave could have been your end. You could have had Lady Alia contact us, but you didn't."

Franc had been upset when I'd described everything that had happened while we'd been separated, but I hadn't understood just how upset until now. "I tried to reach Liam, but you're right. I was excited to handle the quest on my own."

"Was it because you didn't trust us..." His hands ran over my shoulders and down over the globes of my butt before gripping them firmly in each hand. "...to keep you safe?"

"No. I know all of my mates would have been there to protect me."

"Damn right we would have. Do you agree to your punishment?"

I couldn't quite make my mouth form the words, so I nodded in agreement. In one fluid motion, Franc spun me around and sat down on the leather bench, draping me over his lap with my ass up in the air.

Franc's right hand came down on one cheek then the other with a series of smacks that made more heat flow out from under his fingertips into my skin and straight between my legs where wetness gathered once more within moments. He set a steady rhythm across both cheeks that had me rocking back against him with each strike against my flesh. Each slap felt like it connected not just against skin but deep inside as well, awakening sensations within me I'd never experienced before now. My breathing quickened along with the pace of Franc's spanks until finally he stopped, rubbing each spot gently for several seconds.

"You're lucky you're so damn cute." Franc flipped me over and cradled me against him, pulling me in for a kiss. It started off slow, but quickly built into a passionate embrace of lips and tongues. I loved the way he tasted, masculine with a hint of that wild forest scent. His hands found my hips and then slid down over my ass, cupping and rubbing each cheek as we kissed. Franc broke the kiss off first and stood up, pulling me up with him in one fluid motion. I wrapped my arms around his neck as he moved us to the bed and laid me down on it on my back.

Franc pulled off his shirt before crawling over me with a predatory gaze that left no doubt he wouldn't be denied. When Franc's cock slid between my legs, rubbing against my wet folds without entering me yet, I arched up against him in encouragement.

"Please," I begged him with no shame or hesitation in saying what I wanted aloud.

"Please what?" he asked playfully while continuing our slow pace together.

Franc chuckled under his breath at my plea before sliding into me right to the hilt in one long thrust that took my breath away for an instant before he began moving within me again.

"More," I whispered under my breath at first, but then repeated myself louder for him when he kept going slowly despite my pleading for more speed.

"More? More of you?" He smiled wickedly at me as if enjoying this game we played together every bit as much as I did, maybe even more? His thrusts picked up speed little by little until we were moving together faster than before, but still not fast enough for either of us yet. This time around there were no magical beasts or fae mages lurking about trying to take us out or keep us apart. This time it was just us, together, finally getting our chance at love despite fate's best efforts against us.

I felt Franc's hands digging into my hips as he thrust into me. The intensity of his focus, the surety of his movements, and the absolute confidence in his ability to handle me were all new experiences for me. I trusted Franc with everything I had, and that trust extended to this moment between us.

"I want more," I replied. "More of everything."

When Franc leaned down over me, laying on top of me with his full weight as he continued thrusting into me, I wrapped my legs around him, welcoming him deeper within me as I arched up against him to meet his every move.

"You're so damn wet for me," he murmured against my neck.

I looked up at Franc as he continued to thrust into me, taking me higher and higher with each stroke. I was so close I could almost taste it.

"Harder," I pleaded with him.

Franc's smile spread across his face, and then he leaned down to kiss me as he picked up the pace of his thrusts again. One hand slid under my right knee and lifted my leg up against his hip, which hit a new angle within me that had my eyes rolling back in my head for a moment. Franc's free hand gripped my chin, forcing me to look at him again while we moved together.

"You're going to come for me now."

Those words sent a wave of pleasure through me. My body arched up against Franc's as wave after wave of pleasure washed through me, igniting every nerve ending along the way and leaving behind a lingering fire that didn't seem capable of going out or being contained within me anymore. Franc continued thrusting into me, prolonging my orgasm until it finally ebbed away, leaving us both panting for air in its wake.

When he spoke again, Franc's voice was gravelly with exhaustion and satisfaction combined. "You're not quite finished yet." He leaned down over me again and kissed me passionately as he quickened his pace once more, taking us both over the edge once more together within minutes. As we lay there panting for air together afterward, I couldn't help but think about how this might be my new normal. Franc, me, my other mates, together like this, always?

HOUSE LOWE

SERA

I felt Franc's hand sliding up my back, up my spine, and into my hair. He tilted my head back and kissed me, his tongue exploring my mouth, claiming me as his own. I melted against the demi-god of pleasure, letting him take control of me in a way I'd never imagined with anyone before. When he pulled away from the kiss, he left me panting for air but not wanting to break contact with him. He leaned down and whispered in my ear, "That was some incredibly passionate sex. I may have to find a reason to punish you again, mate."

A chuckle bubbled up out of me. "Then I'll need to plan some ways to earn it," I replied under my breath just before Franc scooped me up off the bed like I weighed nothing at all.

He hooked a finger under my chin, forcing me to hold the full intensity of his gaze. "You will keep your safety in mind, Sera, or I'll remind you as often as needed to make the lesson stick."

"Yes, Sir," I quipped back, earning an arched brow

from him. A moment later my stomach rumbled loudly enough for us both to hear it. "Do you remember where the kitchen is?"

He chuckled under his breath then looked at me with a confident grin on his face. "What kind of mate would I be if I didn't know where to get you food?"

Franc lifted me up to my feet and then wrapped my robe around me. We stopped off at the bathroom and cleaned ourselves up, and then he led me out of the bedroom and through the house, pausing along the way to turn on the lights for me. When we got to the kitchen, we discovered Caden hard at work making a pile of waffles.

Franc pulled out a chair for me at the island counter. "Have a seat. Instead of joining you, I'm going to leave you in Caden's capable hands." He leaned in and gave me a lingering goodbye kiss before he turned and left.

I sat down, taking in my surroundings. The kitchen was enormous and had an industrial look to it with contrasting white cabinets, a dark granite countertop, stainless steel appliances, and maple hardwood floors, and black accents along the walls and cabinets. Everything looked new or recently renovated, which definitely fit with Grams aesthetic.

"I'd say good morning, but it looks like you already have that well in hand, I can smell the scent of them on you," Caden said, his eyes flashing red but glinting with humor. "I bet you've worked up an appetite?"

"I got up early eager to explore our new house, but you're right, I've already been waylaid repeatedly."

He winked at me before he placed a plate of waffles in front of me. To my surprise, there was a big scoop of delectable ice cream crowning the stack. "Dig in, little mage. You'll need your energy to keep up with me and the others."

I looked him over, taking in his shirtless frame under that apron, and my mouth went dry. I knew another round with Caden would leave me spent and happy again, and I wasn't that surprised to discover I was interested despite the morning's activities so far.

"The waffles make sense, but ice cream too?" I asked.

"I remember how fond you are of it," Caden said with a wink, "and I think you've earned some spoiling."

I felt the heat rise in my cheeks as I thought back to our last time in a kitchen. "This is so indulgent. Thank you, Caden." I picked up a fork and dug into the gooey deliciousness, the fluffy, crispy waffle pairing decadently with the caramel swirl vanilla ice cream melting into it. "This is a lot of carbs, but I love it."

"Don't mages eat carbs? Like every other species on this planet?" He chuckled under his breath as he worked on finishing up a plate for himself at the island across from me.

"Oh, mages definitely eat carbs. At least, this one does," I replied.

"That's good, because I'm considering quitting my day job and becoming the family chef."

I shook my head as I swallowed another big bite. "No, Caden, I can't let you do that. I know how much you adore your work. Besides, I loved working alongside you in that dreamland and I can't wait to do it again. Just imagine me playing naughty mage at your side as we take down criminals together."

I could see the wheels turning in Caden's mind as he considered the possibilities.

"C'mon, admit it. You loved having me by your side."

Caden sighed. "You know I did, but I don't love putting you in danger. Plus, I know Franc will have it out of my hide if he thinks I'm risking you," Caden replied.

I sat up straight, squirming a little in my seat as I visualized Franc and Caden doing well, half a dozen such things together. "I understand I'm precious to all of you, but I think I've shown I'm able to handle myself." I stuffed another creamy, crunchy bite into my mouth, daring him to argue with me.

"We know that, we do, it's just hard accepting that there's only so much that's reasonable to do with protecting our mate."

I winked at him. "You'll get used to it."

Caden sat down across from me at the island countertop while I continued eating my waffles and ice cream. He looked deep into my eyes and whispered. "I'm looking forward to getting used to a lot of things, Sera. Now, what do you think you'll do now that you have your magic working at full power?"

"I haven't thought that far ahead yet. My head has been spinning from everything that happened these last few days. I need to get over by my shop and see how everything's going. It was good to call Pepper last night and hear her voice, but I need to show my face again."

"Just wait until the sun comes up," Caden replied. "Somehow, I don't see you being satisfied running your coffee shop anymore."

"I've been thinking about that too," I replied. "My magic is so much stronger now, I know I can help people with my abilities. I adore my shop, but I can do so much more. Pepper's used to running it now, anyway. And I can always visit when I need to get my gaming in."

Caden nodded along, listening intently to me as he ate his food. "What kind of magical work do you think you'd enjoy?"

I shrugged, still chewing on my waffle. "Honestly, working in security or investigations was always at the top of my list for what I wanted to do with my life. Something about finding bad guys and protecting those who need it has always appealed to me."

Caden threw his head back and laughed heartily at my admission. "Well, it looks like you have a plan then? I can certainly help you out with that. I'm sure my chief would love having an in with House Lowe." He took a bite of his food, never taking his eyes off me for even a moment.

The way he looked at me, there was a hunger in his eyes that made my core ache for him again, despite how thoroughly we'd already explored our desires together last night. The thrill of anticipation filled the air between us, making the atmosphere crackle with electricity like before a storm rolled in over the horizon. When Caden stood up from his stool and walked around behind me, placing his hands on my shoulders while leaning in close behind me, all thoughts fled from my mind but one: what was Caden going to do next?

"You'll figure it out, and we'll all help you make it happen. Now, have you had enough to eat?" he whispered against my ear. "Because I can't take my eyes off of you and I'm hungry for something more."

My spine tingled with goosebumps as chills ran down it under Caden's touch; every nerve ending awakened by his proximity alone as only an incubus could. But when he spoke those words to me, it was as if an electric shock hit every cell in my body all at once. Every hair on my body stood up straight as an intense heat ran through every inch of flesh from head to toe under Caden's attention. A flash fire ignited between us when our gazes met over my shoulder; there was no denying we both wanted more than simply idle flirtation right now.

"You're right. I'm done eating, and I'm ready for a dessert only you can provide," I said with a confident smile.

"I want you. Now," he whispered, his lips close to my ear.

"So what are you waiting for?" I asked him over my shoulder. "Hurry and get those clothes off already."

Caden didn't waste another moment as he stripped out of his jeans and apron in record time and then stood behind me again. He grasped my hips through my silky robe and pulled me backwards against him, his erection rubbing against the cleft of my ass through my clothing as he leaned forward to nibble on my neck and earlobe while he explored my body with his hands.

"I can smell your arousal from here, Sera. You're so wet for me already, aren't you?" he whispered into my ear as he pinched a nipple through my robe between his fingers while the other hand slid down between my legs to explore further. The pleasure of his touch was almost too much to bear. I hadn't realized how much I would love having multiple partners or how eager they were to explore every inch of me, day after day. "Look at you! You've soaked your panties. You must have been dripping wet when Franc dropped you off here. Are you ready for more?" Caden asked me, rubbing along the length of my pussy through the fabric of my panties while also sliding one finger inside me alongside it.

A cry escaped from my lips at his words and at the sensations flooding over every nerve ending in response to him touching me like this again so soon after my other adventures this morning, yet it felt so right too. Was it possible to be sexually satiated yet still eager for more sex? Perhaps especially now that we were bound by fate, magic, and love?

"Yes! Please?! I feel like I'm about to explode, and I'm not going to last long if you keep that up," I told him. "Please, Caden! I need you inside me. Filling me."

He growled against my ear and then spun me around, pulling the sash of my robe free before throwing it off of me. He then bent me over a nearby countertop island, grasping my hips. "I love how eager you are for me," he said as he ran a hand along the length of my spine, his touch sending shivers down it in response. "I need you so much right now too." He ran his hand back up along my spine until his fingers threaded through the hair at the nape of my neck, tugging it slightly as his other hand grasped my hip and guided himself into me from behind.

The feeling of fullness as he slid home within me hit every pleasure receptor I had like a wave crashing against the shoreline on a stormy night. Caden held still inside of me for a moment while he let both of us adjust to being joined again. Then he pulled back out almost all the way before sliding back home again even faster than before.

"You feel amazing! So tight and wet around me!" With each word out of his mouth, I could feel Caden growing more excited and energetic in his movements. It was as he fed off the energy and mutual desire between us in this intimate moment together.

My body responded to him with each thrust forward with its own wave of pleasure rolling through me. Each new wave building upon itself until I felt myself teetering on the edge of an explosive orgasm that would shake me to my core yet again. Caden's hands gripped tighter on mine where we held onto opposite sides of the countertop island to keep what leverage we could against the slick surface. Little gasps escaped from my lips behind clenched teeth as we moved together faster and faster towards our climaxes together. Every nerve ending in my body was alive with sensation; every inch aware only of Caden's touch against it right now as if nothing else existed beyond us.

Caden's fingers dug into my hips, and he pulled me back against him as he thrust forward, burying himself deep within me. "Come for me, Sera!" he growled out.

With his words, I let out a cry of pleasure as my body exploded in a vast wave of pleasure. Every nerve ending in my body lit up with pleasure at the same time and then all went blissfully blank and sated. A moment later, another wave of pleasure hit me, and then another. I felt like I was floating on the clouds of heaven; smiling blissfully to myself as each wave washed over me anew.

Caden's hands slid up my arms to wrap around my shoulders while he held me close against him while still thrusting into me from behind. His panting breaths tickled the back of my neck. "I loved watching you come apart for me like that! I can't hold out any longer!" He groaned out a few seconds later, his whole body tensing behind me before he released within me with a final few thrusts forward that left us both panting for breath together afterwards.

I turned around within his arms to face him, wrapping my arms around his neck while we held each other close for a moment in silence just enjoying the afterglow together.

"Thank you, Caden," I exclaimed to him between gasping breaths. "I'm going to get used to having you around every day. All of you."

"You'd better, cause I'm not going anywhere," Caden replied. "None of us are." He picked my robe up off the floor and slid it back on over my shoulders, wrapping it around me and cinching the tie around my middle. "You headed back to bed?"

"No, it's almost morning and I'm still intent on exploring this house."

Caden pulled his jeans back on. "I could go with you?"

I leaned in and gave him a kiss on the tip of his nose. "I'll be fine, demon. Besides, everyone else will be up shortly and wanting your waffles. You've got to stay here and play head chef."

Caden threw up his hands, but his smile softened his reaction. "Yes, ma'am, I'll get back to work."

EXPLORING THE GROUNDS

SERA

I took my leave of Caden and wandered through the halls, poking my nose into the various rooms and enjoying the decor. The house had a rustic yet modern feel to it, with clean lines and minimalist furniture. I loved the open spaces, along with the large windows that let in the first rays of morning sunshine. There were plenty of nooks and crannies to explore, and I wondered if they were hiding any secret rooms behind those walls or under floorboards? Knowing Ms. Dara Lowe, plenty.

Halfway down the hallway on my left, I turned into a room that looked part library, part office. They'd lined every wall with bookshelves full of books, most of them with arcane symbols on the spines. I checked out the room's decor, impressed by the hand carved wooden shelves and cabinets that lined every wall. The left wall had a large desk and chair, with a matching bookcase built in behind it. The right wall had a fireplace flanked by floor to ceiling windows, which I assumed looked out over the backyard. A fire would be so pleasant right now.

The middle of the room held two overstuffed chairs facing each other beside a low table covered in a collection of what looked like tarot cards and other fortune telling trinkets. "Wow, my Grams has some serious crafty nerd cred!" I exclaimed out loud to myself, smiling at my joke as I admired her collection of books on mage craftsmanship and spell casting. There were even some on demonology! "I'm so going to have to take notes here!" I told myself as I walked up to one shelf full of books on demonology and pulled out one titled How To Banish A Demon 101: Tips from a Mage's Perspective. "This will be fun reading. I wonder if Caden would find it useful?"

"I have something else for you to read," Emrys said from the doorway.

I spun around, surprised to see him there, rubbing a hand over his beard as his gaze roamed hungrily over me.

I crossed the room to where he stood. "What do you have for me?"

"I'm always ready to deliver for you, Sera," he drawled, biting his lip. So presumptuous, but I wouldn't take Emrys any other way. He held up two envelopes. "Today, I'm role playing your mail carrier."

I took the envelopes from Emrys, and he moved in close behind me wrapping his arms around my waist. I arched into him, loving his attention. "So what are these?"

He kissed the back of my neck. "The first one is a job assignment from your grandmother."

I rolled my eyes. "Of course it is. Wait, are you reading my mail?"

He shook his head, his beard tickling the sensitive

skin of my neck. "No, I'm just repeating what the courier told me, that it was your next assignment 'for your review.'"

I couldn't help but pout a little. "I suppose I knew this was coming, but I haven't even been back a full day yet. You'd think it could wait a week?"

Emrys chuckled against my neck, sending chills down my spine. "I'm sure you can open it later. You've earned some flexibility from the old dame."

"I wouldn't let her hear you call her old." I sighed and turned around within his arms so we were face to face, which was when I saw the second envelope in his hand. My heart skipped a beat as I took it from him and read the return address, recognizing the florid script: "Mom? It's been years since we last spoke!"

Emrys shrugged but remained silent, so I continued talking to myself out loud as I opened up the letter and skimmed it.

Dear Sera,

Your grandmother has informed me you've learned of your father's faery heritage. I'm sorry I kept it a secret from you, but as Grams said, I had my reasons.

I'm so happy to know you've found your place in the world. I hope you'll be able to forgive me for being absent from your life for so long. Your grandmother has invited me to visit and I hope that you'll extend me the same courtesy. Perhaps we could even discuss your father.

I look forward to seeing you again, my darling daughter.

All My Love, Mom

A tear slipped down my cheek, and Emrys swiped it away with his thumb. "What's wrong?" he asked in a gentle tone.

"Nothing bad. She says she's coming for a visit!" I whispered, clutching the letter close to my chest as if it might vanish at any moment.

"Oh, that's wonderful!" he exclaimed, wrapping his arms around me and pulling me back against him again.

When Emrys pulled back enough to look me in the eye, I felt like he was looking right into my soul and could see every part of me laid bare before him. It was both humbling and empowering at the same time. He held onto my shoulders as if he wanted to say something more, but then hesitated before continuing with a smile on his face like he had an idea or thought brewing in his mind that he wasn't sharing with me yet.

"You've lived separately from the supe community for so long." He leaned forward then kissed my cheek before continuing on. "Dara seems intent on putting your mage skills to work for the family business right away. Are you ready for that?"

I looked into his dark brown eyes, and realized he wasn't doubting my ability to step up, just asking if I wanted to. I knew the answer.

"I've never been one to sit back and wait on life to

happen for me, Emrys. Now that I have control over my magic, I'm eager to flex my mage muscles." I bit my lip, glancing away from the intensity in his gaze, taking in the immense library around us before looking back. "Will my mates support me? Will you support me? Because there's going to be an element of risk in any job. I can't imagine Franc will, not after what he said earlier."

Emrys placed his hands on my shoulders. "I will. Heck, we'll all support you in your career. Even Franc. Even if it's dangerous. It's a part of who you are, and it's a life you've waited far too long to start."

"You're not worried about my safety? That's all the others have gone on about this morning."

I felt Emrys' wry smile all the way into my toes. "They're just rebounding over the recent stressful events, which they'll get over. I, for one, am not worried about you. I've brought you back from the brink of death once, and I'll do it again."

I let out a laugh over his dark humor. "Your overconfidence is reassuring, but infectious. You may have to spend some time convincing the others."

"I'd be happy to, mate. Now," he said, a wicked glint in his eyes, "can I show you what I found?"

I nodded and then accepted his hand. Emrys led me out of the library, down a corridor, and outside through a pair of arched, tall glass-paned French doors. The early-morning sunlight seemed to sparkle with energy. The scent of fresh grass and blooming flowers hung in the air. I could feel the life of the garden seeping into my pores, rejuvenating me after the long night. I turned a circle, taking in all the beauty around me.

He gestured to the tall grasses, which were swaying in

the wind despite there being no breeze where we stood in the middle of the garden. I reached out with my mage sight and gasped at what I saw. The plants were alive with magical energy!

"This is amazing!" I exclaimed, throwing my arms out wide. The sun warmed my skin, and a light breeze blew against my hair, causing it to fan out around me. "I've never seen anything like it, especially not in the heart of the city."

"I bet Dara gifted you this property knowing how your mage and faery magics would recharge just by a walk in these gardens," Emrys said.

He took my hand, and I let him lead me through the tall grasses. They swayed back and forth in the magical breeze, tickling my legs. When we reached the center of a circle of standing stones, Emrys stopped and turned back to me. "I thought you'd like to see this place. The energy here feels different from the rest of the gardens."

I felt the energy of the stones all around us, and I had to wonder if that was what made me feel so light-headed. Like I was floating on air.

"Are these enchanted?" I asked, my voice little more than a whisper.

"It feels that way," Emrys nodded. "The moment I came across this, I knew I had to show it to you," he explained.

"There's something different about this place. The energy feels... cleaner? More pure? Grams must have built this."

Emrys smiled at my observation and then held out his hand to me again. "It might even be older than that. There's more."

I didn't hesitate before taking his hand in mine and following him through the grasses until we reached the center of the circle of standing stones. The stones were slightly taller than Emrys and spaced evenly apart around the circle with enough space between them for us to walk through without brushing against them. The closest stone was just a few feet away from where we stood.

Each stone was roughly oval in shape and covered with etched markings that seemed familiar yet foreign at the same time. Looking closely at one of them, I realized they were runes from an ancient dialect of mage language that I hadn't learned yet in my studies.

"Thank you for showing me this."

When I looked up again, Emrys was standing right in front of me. He ran his hands down my arms, his eyes full of desire as he leaned forward and placed a kiss on my neck right below my earlobe while his hands continued down my sides until he gripped my hips and pulled me close against him with a groan. His considerable erection was unmistakable against my belly as he pressed forward against me with slow movements that had me panting within moments.

"You smell so good, Sera Lowe," he murmured against my skin as he moved along my neck towards my jawline with soft kisses and gentle nibbles along the way.

I tilted my head back and closed my eyes as wave after wave of pleasure washed over me from both his words and his touch alone. He ran his hands up along my sides over the silky fabric of my robe until he reached the underside of my breasts just as he slipped his tongue into my mouth. The sensation shot straight to between my legs, making them feel heavy. When Emrys pulled back, I wanted to cry out at being denied more contact with him, but then he whisked off the sash holding up the front of my robe open in one swift movement before sliding it off over my shoulders and dropping it onto the mossy ground. I felt the energy of the stones all around us, and I had to wonder if that was what made me feel so light-headed.

My breath caught in my throat as I stood there, naked under Emrys' gaze. His eyes raked over me, lingering on my breasts. I arched my back, and he growled low in his throat.

"You're stunning," he murmured as he reached out to me and ran a reverent finger down my neck along the line of my collarbone. I shivered at his touch, eager for more of him. More of everything he had to offer me. "I've wanted since you first walked into my magical ethics class back at Goldenbriar, Sera Lowe."

My heart thrummed in surprise at his words. In this moment there were no games or coy flirtations from Emrys; just raw honesty from a man who didn't seem to know how to hide his desires from me. It was refreshingly honest, and it made me want him even more than I already did.

"Now you have me, mate. What are you going to do with me?" I asked breathlessly as a wave of desire washed through me at the intensity in his gaze when he looked at me like that. Like I was everything he wanted.

He said nothing else as he slipped off his shoes and then his shirt before unbuckling and shedding down his jeans without ever taking his eyes off mine or moving closer to me again until they fell onto the ground moments later. When Emrys stood before me naked in all of his glory, all thoughts fled from my mind besides how much I wanted him.

"You are so damn sexy right now. You take my breath away with your beauty, Sera Lowe," Emrys said huskily as he walked forward towards me again until we stood toe-to-toe again pressed against each other body-to-body. Time lost meaning here among these stones when I could feel the energy coursing through every nerve ending in my body just by being near him like this again.

His hands moved to my hips, and he pulled me forward against him until the head of his erection slid along the wet folds of my sex. I gasped at the contact and all but begged him to take me. "Please, Emrys."

He groaned in reply before he leaned forward, hooking his arms under my knees, and then swept me off my feet. I wrapped my arms around his neck and held on tight as he walked into the center of the circle. I felt a tingling sensation wash over me that made me shiver with anticipation for what was to come between us. When we reached the center stone, Emrys sat down on it with a grunt and then slid back until his hips were laying flat against it. He pulled me forward again until I straddled his lap, facing him with our faces inches apart again.

"I want you so much right now, Sera."

"I'm never letting you go, Emrys," I replied breathlessly as I thrust myself down onto Emrys' length in a movement that had us both moaning at our joining in mutual blissful ecstasy. The gardens and the standing stones heightened the wave of pleasure washing over us, leaving me breathless.

We didn't need words after that; only actions filled with passion-fueled abandonment as we reveled in our newfound bliss alone in each other's arms out here under nature's canopy away from everything else around us, except for these stones watching over us from their silent perches surrounding our secluded glen.

I was the first to come, crying out my pleasure into the night air. Moments later, Emrys tensed beneath me and then let out a roar. His seed flooded me as I milked him for every drop he had to offer me. The moment passed, and we laid there panting against each other until our breathing slowed back down to normalcy again. At that moment, I couldn't imagine anywhere else I'd rather be than together with my mates, building our future together.

"I feel like I could stay here with you forever," Emrys whispered, his breath fanning against my neck.

When Emrys stomach growled, I let out a giggle. "I may have forgotten to mention Caden has a pile of waffles cooked up."

"In that case," Emrys rolled over, going in search of our clothes. "I'm putting forever on hold until after breakfast."

He handed me my robe, and I stood up and pulled it on. "Since when are you my sensible guy?" I asked.

He pulled on his jeans and then winked at me. "Waffles trump sensible, mate. Every time."

***

Thank you so much for reading Devoted Desires, the last chapter in the Stolen Legacy series! It would mean a lot to me if you could leave a review. A single line or two makes a big difference for other people when deciding if a book is a good fit for them.

As a special bonus to you, I've got a bonus epilogue which gives another peek at Taneisha and Raymond's story.
There are three bonuses for this mini-side series (all free for you to download via the links below):
Looted Legacies
Hidden Hearts Bonus Epilogue
Devoted Desires Bonus Epilogue
Or,
Visit candicebundy.com/bonus-content to see all available freebies.

ALSO BY CANDICE BUNDY

The Stolen Legacy Series

Looted Legacies, A prequel novella

Forbidden Fates

Entangled Essence

Hidden Hearts

Reckless Rapture

Sworn Spirits

Devoted Desires

The Shadow Series

Shadow in the City, A prequel novella

Twinned Shadow

Poisoned Shadow

Shadow Underground

Caught Between Worlds Series

Smoke and Daemons

(previously published as Daemon Whisperer)

Other Works

Ripples, a novella

Open Rack, a contemporary short

WRITING AS CR BUNDY

The Depths of Memory Series

The Dream Sifter

Dreams Manifest

For a list of my full catalog of available titles, visit my
<u>candicebundy.com/books</u> page.

ALSO BY PIPER FOX

Academy for Reapers: Paranormal Romance

Big Wolf on Campus Series: Wolf Shifter Football Romances

The Stolen Legacy Series: Paranormal Reverse Harem

Midnight Huntress Series: Paranormal Reverse Harem

Alien Warriors of New Dilaria Series: Sci-Fi Reverse Harem

The Ironhaven Pack Series: Wolf Shifter Romances

The Dragon Space Order Bride Series: Sci-Fi Romance

<u>Bears of Crooked Creek</u>: A Bear Shifter Romance Series

<u>Seven Brides For Seven Demons</u>: A Demon Romance Series

<u>Last Warriors of Dilaria</u>: A Sci-Fi Romance Series

The Immortal Blood Series: Vampire Romance

ABOUT CANDICE BUNDY

Candice lives in Denver, Colorado with her son and their cat Newt. A professional hedonist, rabble-rouser, winemaker, and goat-herder, she adores archeology and mythology. Candice focuses on habit hacking to meet minimalist, health, productivity, and positive mojo goals, and sometimes even blogs about it. An unrepentant epicurean, she grows heirloom tomatoes and ferments a variety of sauerkraut, sourdough, kombucha, pickles, and water kefir.

If you would like to know when she has new books out, please sign up for her newsletter here. Email her if the mood strikes you.

For more information:
candicebundy.com
candice@candicebundy.com

ABOUT PIPER FOX

Piper Fox writes steamy paranormal romances for sassy, strong-willed women and the sexy, alpha men who love them.

Follow her on:
Facebook: facebook.com/PiperFoxAuthor
Bookbub: https://www.bookbub.com/profile/piper-fox